POINT OF CONTENTION

Louisa Neil

MENAGE AMOUR

Siren Publishing, Inc.
www.SirenPublishing.com

A SIREN PUBLISHING BOOK
IMPRINT: Ménage Amour

POINT OF CONTENTION

ISBN-10: 1-61034-621-1
ISBN-13: 978-1-61034-621-4

First Printing: May 2011

Cover design by Jinger Heaston

Printed in the U.S.A.

PUBLISHER
Siren Publishing, Inc.
www.SirenPublishing.com

DEDICATION

For my husband, my erotic muse.

AUTHOR'S NOTE

Agrarian: Relating to land or the ownership or division of land.
—*Webster's New World Dictionary*

POINT OF CONTENTION

LOUISA NEIL

Prologue

From the office window, he watched her long legs as she jogged the path on the far side of the compound. The distance gave him perspective he knew he desperately needed. She was off limits to him in all ways. "Hell," he said aloud, "she's Travis's woman, hands off!" How many times in the last months had he told himself the same thing and none of the times did it help. The fact that he'd locked his door and was now fisting his cock at the sight of her was completely out of character for him.

Until now, if he saw a woman and was interested, he approached, made his pitch, and worked with the results. Most times, he wound up spending time with the woman in question, and a few times he'd been rejected. But he'd always made the contact. It was so out of the norm for him to covet this woman that he'd resorted to masturbating to her image as she exercised within his view. His thighs ached holding his weight while he stood beside the window making the rhythmic motions. Stuart got a strange feeling of forbiddance about the act he was practicing, yet the thrill offset the need to stop, rather prompted him to continue until he shot his load, capturing most of it in his palm and reaching for the tissues to clean himself.

The fact that they hadn't met yet was just one more unexplainable side to his feelings. He'd put off the inevitable as long as he could.

While he hadn't acknowledged the idea to anyone verbally, he knew the timing of his last trip was carefully planned to coincide with her arrival. Giving her and Travis time to settle in together was important to both of them. He moved back to his desk chair and grabbed his coffee mug, the liquid now cold. The papers scattered on the desktop before him were a blur of numbers and letters. None of it interested him, hadn't since the decision was made to offer Kadence the one-year contract as pastry chef for Agrarian Lodge. Now it was too late to change his mind, even if it meant his sanity. Forcing himself, he focused on the work before him, anything to take his mind off her.

Since his return last night, he'd read her employment papers twice more, the photograph attached now imprinted on his brain. With a resigned sigh, he knew he'd memorized it the first time he'd seen it. While it was a stodgy passport type, he'd taken one look at her and his heart had slammed against his chest wall. Her dark hair was pulled back from her face, and she wore no makeup. There was no smile for the camera, only a full face picture. It should have been ordinary, but it wasn't. That was part of his problem. The woman staring back at him from the print was anything but ordinary even in two dimensions.

He understood how Travis had become enamored by her, even though their relationship was long distance and, as he kept reinforcing, just platonic friends. In the more than ten years he'd known Travis, he understood "female friends" wasn't a term the other man embraced. He was a hands-on kind of guy, not one to shy away from physical contact. That was great, for it worked for Travis. He held no illusions of long-term stability. He was more of a flash-and-burn kind of guy, using up all the emotion he carried in a short time and becoming bored quickly. Kadence "Kay" Farrell was the exception.

With a pronounced sigh, he mentally decided that if she was as good a pastry chef as reported, that was all that would matter. After all, his business was taking care of his guests, and with the remote setting of the lodge, meals were a large part of the entertainment. So this afternoon, he'd attend the regular Wednesday afternoon supervisors' meeting and finally meet her. Hopefully, she'd get out of his brain, allowing him to return to some level of efficiency he used to know. He'd imagined that she spoke with a lisp or had a cackle laugh that grated on his nerves. Anything to break the strain of his unabashed lust for the woman his best friend was in love with. A woman he'd never met and was now locked into working with for the next twelve months.

He knew a year was a long time to ache for a woman, especially if she was so close at hand—hand being his operative word. He shook his head at the concept that he'd spend the next months tugging on his cock for sexual satisfaction instead of being buried deep inside her pussy or ass. A shiver ran through him when he contemplated how she'd suck him off, if she'd swallow his length down her throat. Laughing aloud, he said, "Maybe she doesn't suck cock," but he sobered quickly, remembering she'd kept Travis enamored for two years. This woman had to have something special to keep his attention. Stuart wondered if he'd ever find out for himself.

Chapter One

"If you're not the lead dog, the view never changes."
—Anonymous

Sun-warmed and physically exhausted, Kadence stood under the shower spray, the hot water erasing some of the exertion and stress. It would be silly to be nervous about meeting her new employer, yet there was an air of apprehension around her as she dressed. The move had gone easier than planned, all her belongings unboxed in their new home. Or at least what she'd brought with her. The rest was in storage in a facility in New Jersey. For now, her clothes and favorite books were all she would need. Her position as pastry chef for the Agrarian Lodge had many perks. Her two-room apartment was one, as well as all her meals. Meals she would now be in charge of, some of the time. Pulling on clean chinos and a soft pink T-shirt, she added a hint of mascara and tinted her lips red with a gloss. Comfortable sneakers were tied in place, and she was ready for her second managers' meeting.

Last week, she'd sat in and gotten a feel for how the place was run. This week, she had her menus ready as well as a few small requests. Today, she'd finally get to meet the infamous Stuart Drake, owner of the lodge. For the two years she'd been friends with Travis Polson, she'd heard a lot about Stuart and even seen a photograph of him. The e-mail had been sent when the lodge was first opened and Travis had given her his new address. His enthusiasm for the lodge and his new job running the kitchen was apparent, the picture reinforcing his words of his best buddy and longtime friend.

Only the moment she saw them, their arms locked around each other's shoulders as they stood before the newly hung sign, Kay realized there was something about Mr. Drake that drew her to him. Maybe it was the dark eyes and black wavy hair that was just a bit too long to be called conventional. Or maybe it was the close-clipped beard that covered his cheeks and chin. Maybe it was the look of defiance for the camera that had made her catch a breath, his arrogance pronounced, as if he were inviting a confrontation. Whatever it had been, a quick glance had turned her insides warm, something that hadn't happened to her in a long time.

A crazy thought passed through her at the time that it would be interesting to be in the middle of those two men, sandwiched between their solid bodies. She could almost feel the texture of their skin against her fingers. She knew Travis had a smooth chest and decided that Stuart would have soft curls of dark chest hair. She also assumed the curls would lead down his belly, forming a halo of curls around the base of his cock. She'd spent several nights using dildos and dongs as replacements for the men's cocks, imagining how they'd love her. She dreamed all sorts of wonderful scenarios, imagining how their bodies would intertwine and the logistics of their positions. Each time, she would finish exhausted and sated from their touch.

Surprisingly, her fantasies were the one hesitation that kept presenting itself while she mulled over the offered contract. By way of Travis, she knew Stuart was single and had never been married. She also knew they had been best friends since their days of the baseball farm team they'd both played on. She'd begun to wonder if the friends had shared women in their younger days.

Kay knew Stuart could be dangerous to her on a level she hadn't known before. While she'd seen chemistry in action many times, she herself had opted for a combination of respect and friendship for her first husband. They had dated for a long time, knew each other well, and when the time was right, got married. What she thought was love turned out to be companionship, and it wasn't enough for either of them. She'd wanted love and lust, hot and erotic, from Eric, but what she'd gotten was a tepid version of sexual companionship. Once the newness and excitement of the wedding was behind them, their jobs and day-to-day life had tarnished their existence. Three years later Kay still wondered how she'd talked herself into marrying him. The answer was always the same—Eric was what she thought she wanted. Professional, yes, athletic, yes, handsome, God yes, especially with his beach-bum attitude, blond hair, and blue eyes.

In the beginning, all he had to do was look at her with those soft ocean blue eyes and she'd melt. Only after being together for two years did she realize she wasn't the only one he looked at like that. That was his downfall in her eyes. Kay felt she was worth his full attention and wouldn't accept his casual dalliances, as he called them. He claimed they meant nothing to him and were just a sexual outlet. She drew a breath and let it out slowly, letting the image of Eric fade. He was long gone, and she had a new life to begin. Without a second glance, she forced herself from the mirror and took one last look around her new home. It was clean and comfortable; the small sitting room and larger bedroom with en suite bath more than met her needs for the time being.

* * * *

The staff was gathering around the large table set in the windowed alcove of the restaurant kitchen in the main lodge. Coffee was brewing, and tea was steeping. Travis was discussing baseball with Hoyt, the lodge's foreman. Lisa, who ran the lodge for Stuart as his office manager, was scanning computer printouts, a glass of cola in front of her. Martha sat quietly with her knitting, her fingers moving the soft wool over the needles, the metal clanking softly, keeping her rhythm. Kay dropped her notes at the far end of the table and disappeared to the other end of the kitchen, using the time to take a few deep breaths for control as she organized pastries on a platter for presentation. She forced herself not to look up when she heard him enter, the screen door snapping shut behind him.

"Stuart, how was your trip?"

Kay listened to the five longtime friends and employees talk with her new boss. Grabbing a glimpse of him, she forced herself to count to ten while she willed her hands to stop shaking. Standing in front of the coffeemaker, the simple act of pouring the hot liquid into a mug made her wonder what his hands might feel like against her skin. It was a sobering thought that made her laugh aloud. "Get a grip," she whispered to herself before she turned to join the others. The sight of him in a flannel shirt with the cuffs folded back and worn denims was enough to push her over the edge. His battered boots and beyond broken in oilskin hat completed the picture. Thankfully, he'd dropped his hat on a counter before taking his place at the head of the table. If he'd left it on, she couldn't guarantee swooning wouldn't be next.

She remembered the billboard and magazine ads she'd grown up with of the Marlboro Man. Now a younger version of that character was standing just a few yards away, and Kay wanted to touch him. "I'm losing my mind," she told herself quietly, her fingers literally itching to stroke his cheek and feel his beard. The vision that fueled her teenage fantasies was within reach. And technically, she had no right to think about him in any way, let alone actually approach him on a sexual level. After all, he was her boss, and this job was important to her. Proving she was capable of doing her new job was important on many levels, mainly to herself.

Not disappointing Travis was high on her list. Not making a fool of herself was higher. Starting over took courage and determination, and she'd succeeded, so far. Losing her concentration for a momentary tryst wasn't wise. Best she focus on the job at hand and forget her hormones. Besides, her cowboy fantasy man would probably like to have a say in the matter. The idea of pleading her case to him flashed through her mind, and she held back a confident smile. Maybe someday she'd let her guard down, but not yet. Not until she'd proven herself. Kadence knew one thing about her own personality—she could be a stubborn bitch when needed. And apparently, Stuart Drake would test her resolve. She checked the platter once more and wondered if he had a current girlfriend.

The old white Labrador that followed behind him dropped by his side. She'd met the dog last week and was quickly becoming attached to him, only to realize this morning he was absent from his perch on the back stairway when she came in to start the baking. Every morning since she'd arrived, the old hound was waiting for her, and every morning she had an ear rub for him.

Kay moved to the far end of the seating and placed the platter of pastries in the center, leaving to retrieve a stack of plates and napkins she'd set aside earlier. When everyone had listened to Mr. Drake's minimal description of his absence, she settled in beside Martha and across from Travis. Only then did she let herself openly appraise her boss. His beard was heavier than in the picture and his eyes darker. His longer hair brushed his collar in a soft wave. When his left hand moved, she followed its path to his forehead, where his fingers wove through his hair, pulling it back from his face. Of course, that was the moment he chose to meet her eyes. For one terrifyingly long second, she froze, forgetting to breathe. He recovered first and smiled with a soft nod.

"I'll assume you're Kadence Farrell?" he asked, his voice deeper than she expected.

"Kay is preferable," she managed to answer without her voice cracking.

"Welcome to Lodge, Kay. Are you settled in, anything you need?"

"Thank you, I'm fine. Martha and Lisa have been wonderful in making me comfortable."

"Let us know if you need anything." Stuart caught her gaze and didn't elaborate any further. Instead, she watched as he looked away, the folder in front of him a good diversion. While he talked with Hoyt about the grounds, she tried to stop watching his hands. They were large hands, with strong, thick fingers. Kay felt the heat rise from her chest to her neck and onto her cheeks when she thought about how his fingers might bring her to a release. Holding back a nervous giggle, she rose and grabbed a coffeepot, topping off the cups on the table. Composed by the time she'd finished, Kay forced herself to not look in his direction. She became very interested in her notes, reinforcing the importance of her job.

They were given a rundown on next week's guests, and their wish lists were circulated. It was a practice Travis had started when he took the job as main chef. Since the lodge was so secluded, each group of guests was forwarded a questionnaire in advance of their arrival. It helped to design the meals for their stay as well as head off any minor or major disasters. Peanuts were one such disaster, depending on the degree of allergy. Alcohol was another. Some groups preferred a dry week, while others preferred an all-out vacation bash for their time at the lodge. Dislikes were strictly adhered to, and Travis was currently laughing at the fact that he'd never had a chance to cook liver and onions for a group yet. Even Kay made a face at his remark, her stomach clenching at the idea of liver, the smell of it cooking making her shudder.

Chapter Two

Stuart listened to Travis talk, but watched Kay from under his lashes. He saw her visibly pale when liver was discussed and held back a smile. A woman he could love, he thought, then quickly dismissed the idea from his mind. Today, she looked different to him. Gone was the severe hairdo. Instead, her sable locks fell in soft waves around her shoulders, reaching to her waist. Her brown eyes seemed tinged with gold rims as the sun teased through the window before her. Worst of all, her voice got to him on a gut level. She reminded him of a blues singer, all gravelly voiced, low and strong with a hint of sex thrown in. Her laugh was sultry and honest, no high-pitched squeals here, just a smooth roll of sound.

She was rapidly getting on his last nerve just sitting there when she rose from her seat and reached to the platter, handing it to Travis to choose from. In doing so, her T-shirt pulled against her breasts, outlining her full shape as it smoothed to a slim waist. He hardened immediately and looked away, only to see Travis watching her, too. And there was the rub. Reminding himself that she was his best friend's dream woman, he pulled the meeting back to order. When all the business was winding down and he thought to slip away, Kay broke in before they would disband.

"I have two quick questions." All eyes were instantly on her, and he watched as she swallowed hard, the instant acknowledgment and embarrassment turning her cheeks pink. "The patch of land just outside the back kitchen entrance, Travis mentioned it was designated as a garden. Whose toes would I be stepping on if I wanted to throw in a few seeds?" Everyone looked to another and back to her, none taking responsibility.

"I told her if she wanted the space I don't see a problem," Hoyt started, "but in all honesty I don't have time to put a man on it."

"I told her the same thing. You know me and getting dirt under my nails." Travis added, "Motor oil is a different subject." He smiled and glanced at Lisa, and she only nodded to him, their private joke not shared with the rest of the group.

"I'll take responsibility for the garden." Straightening in her seat, she added, "I'd just like to put a few rows of herbs and maybe some tomatoes for sauce. Would that be a problem?"

"I don't see it being a major hassle," Stuart started and then turned to Hoyt. "How much time would it take to keep it up if she got it started?"

"Probably a few hours twice a week, but I'm not sure I have the manpower right now, at least until we're finished thinning the new acreage and the fields are planted."

"*No*, I don't want somebody else to tend it. If I start a garden, I'll be responsible for it, completely." Her voice rose just enough to enter the conversation, reminding them she was still there.

"Somehow, while I feel you have good intentions…do you realize how much work it really takes to keep a garden going?" Stuart studied her openly and realized she was doing the same. Her manner and tone changed, and he saw a hint of the lawyerly presence she must have exuded in her previous career.

"I have a general idea, Mr. Drake, or I wouldn't have brought up the prospect. I'll take full responsibility for the project. And just to clarify, I'm not asking for an acre of cleared land, just a space for a few rows of herbs." She held his eye and refused to look away or even blink.

"Then take it, it's all yours. The way I see it, the worst that can happen is you get it started and lose interest. We'll let it turn back to seed and turn it under in the fall."

"You don't have high expectations," she mumbled, a little too loud to be completely under her breath. “May I use some of the hand tools from the gardening shed, Hoyt, or should I buy a set to keep up here?”

“I’ll have one of the men turn up the soil later in the week. From there it’s all yours, Kay.” He met her look and shrugged one shoulder. “There are some duplicate hand tools in the shed. I’ll gather what we have as spares so you can keep them up here at the lodge. If you need supplies, check the garden shed behind the kennels. The rest is up to you.”

“Thank you. I’ll take over once the soil is tilled.” She winked at Hoyt by way of thanks, Stuart decided. His lips started to pull into a smile, and he pulled it back.

“Good luck to you, I hope you know what you’re doing,” Hoyt added, before nodding to the rest of the group and excusing himself back to work. He paused in the doorway, watching the rest of the exchange between his boss and the new lady chef.

“You had a second question?” Stuart asked.

“I don’t want to make trouble for myself or them, so somebody better tell me what’s the deal with the dogs in the kennel. Are they strictly for hunting, or are they pets too?” Stuart heard Hoyt walk out, listening to the screen door catch.

After his return from his trip, Hoyt had discussed with him her questioning about visiting the horses, and he had approved. “I told her outright you were possessive about your dogs and I didn’t want to overstep my authority. I asked her to speak to you about them.” Hoyt had shuffled his feet, uncomfortable with the conversation. “I’ve noticed she stayed away from the kennel. I suppose she’ll talk to you about them.”

Stuart hoped she’d come out with some outrageous request, but asking if his dogs were pets wasn’t it. He’d known Harley wasn’t in his usual spot this morning when he got up and was surprised. His week away seemed to have changed the order of the dog’s life. As dogs went, Harley was a good one, trained to respond to his commands. They'd been together for six years, and this was the first morning he'd woken to find him missing from his doorway, though he'd showed up minutes later.

"They're trained for hunting, but we consider them pets." Stuart's answer didn't clarify anything for Kay.

"Right, got that, but am I allowed to visit them, or should I avoid them?" She stared at him openly before continuing. "I know some people are very fussy about their hunting dogs. I don't want to domesticate them if you're—"

"The dogs are allowed to be petted, Ms. Farrell. I'd prefer you not feed them table scraps, but if you want to spend time with them, I don't have a problem." He hesitated then added, "Unless we have hunters here for the week. Most of the die-hard hunters will bring their own dogs, and I prefer mine to stay sequestered from guests' pets."

"So it's not a problem to visit them occasionally?"

"No, feel free to socialize with them."

"Thanks." She looked back at her notes, pretending to reread them, Stuart noted, while the rest of the group disbanded around her. She smiled at Martha's compliments about her pastries and handed off a tray ready to go to the employee's area for their dessert tonight. He watched her carefully gather her notes before glancing at her watch. He figured she'd bolt now that the meeting was over, but she paused to ask Travis if he needed help getting supper started.

Stuart left quickly when their conversation became an ingredient list. His nerves started to settle leaving her with Travis in the kitchen. The only real consideration he should be having was that she was competent in the kitchen and able to do the job at hand. His mind continued to wonder if her skills moved to the bedroom. If someone looked closely, they would realize he was wearing the strangest grin.

Self-preservation had him conjuring images of her disjointed and uncomfortable in the bedroom. In reality, he noted how she moved easily, with a flowing gait. He hoped deep inside, she'd be amazing in his bed, fiery and verbal, able to tell him what she wanted and needed from him. In return, he'd show her how he could bring her body to orgasm and what it would take to allow his climax. It had been a long time since he'd taken a lover. Stuart knew Kay wasn't a good choice, but he couldn't help himself. Something about her had him envisioning them pressed up against the counter, her pants pulled down around her ankles as he fucked her pussy from behind. The counter would be the perfect height for her to brace herself and absorb his thrusts. His hands itched to feel the weight of her breasts in his palms, to roll her nipples between his fingers. His cock stirred under the taut denim he wore, and he refrained from repositioning it for comfort.

* * * *

Kay stayed for another hour helping the kitchen staff get ready for the evening meal before heading outside. She sat on the back steps, staring down at the patch of land she'd asked to take responsibility for. In her mind, a few herbs and some tomatoes didn't seem like a big deal. Only now, Stuart Drake had turned it into a point of contention. While she'd visualized spending an occasional lazy hour picking a stray weed or two, it was rapidly becoming so much more. Never liking tests, she tried to envision the situation differently and couldn't at first. He'd given her what she asked for and now she felt obligated to make it the best damn garden Mr. Drake had seen in years. Laughing at the silliness of her thoughts, she decided to keep it small, very small this first season, just for herself. If she liked it and was still around next season, maybe she'd enlarge it, but for now, small and manageable was in order. With that perspective fresh on her mind, she was feeling the renewed hope for her dream garden. Hell, maybe she would add a row of flowers just to annoy him!

* * * *

Her days had finally found a routine again, and thankfully this one seemed in sync with her natural body rhythms. She was an early riser, always full of energy. But by ten she was starting to lag. Kay found that by being in the kitchen before five, she had the place all to herself for an hour before the rest of the staff arrived to start breakfast. That hour alone, the silence especially, thrilled her, spurring her on to be creative. By noon, she had changed clothes and done her run. The compound, as the staff called it, was over a thousand acres. Roughly that worked out to be a square two miles in each direction. If she ran part of the perimeter, it was a strong four-mile run. After that, she'd collapse for an hour, her nap a luxury she'd not known since her law school days. By two, she was up and in the shower, refreshed and renewed. The afternoons were her private time. While she usually stopped by the kitchen to make sure there were no problems with her responsibilities, the rest of the day and night was hers. Except Sundays. That was Travis's day off. She oversaw the large buffet brunch that was served just before the guests were loaded into various transports and sent home. For the rest of the day, the staff cleaned and polished. By late afternoon, they were all off duty.

* * * *

Agrarian Lodge was closed to the public on Mondays. It was Mr. Drake's first rule of running the place. Everybody got a second day off scattered throughout the week. When Travis had first sent her the information about his new position, she'd been happy for him. Now that she was here and experiencing it for herself, she was happy for herself, too. What a jewel of a job she'd fallen into. Meeting Travis when she did was a gift from God.

Sitting on an overturned five-gallon plastic bucket, she petted each of the eight beagles that lived in the pen. The space was large even by her standards, and the dogs were playful and well taken care of. While she'd seen hunters' dogs that were kept slim to chase their prey, these dogs were healthy. Kay missed having a pet these past years. These could easily become her surrogates. It was one of the first things she noticed when she visited last winter. Her weekend at the lodge had been more of an interview than a vacation. Kay had spent the two and a half days getting to know the place and the key people she might work with.

Lisa had been welcoming but professional. She was the office manager and responsible for the day-to-day workings of the lodge. Overseeing the domestic staff as well as controlling the reservation desk, she was efficient beyond words. She also seemed lonely, but in a self-imposed way. Not being able to put her finger on why, Kay decided Lisa had a right to her private life and her quiet reserve.

Martha, on the other hand, could talk your ear off in a grandmotherly way. She was responsible for the staff quarters and their meals. She oversaw the male bunkhouse, the female residence house, and the four apartments over the large garage. The staff meals were served in the large kitchen of the women's residence. The living room held a huge flat-screen television and several comfortable seating areas. A pool table stood in the far corner as well as a few game tables scattered around. Upstairs, the female employees had rooms. Rooms that Martha made sure were strictly off limits to men, any men. She reminded Kay of a retired army drill sergeant at times, but touched her with her understanding of others. A rare woman, indeed. Spending time with her was always educational in various ways depending on Martha's mood.

Hoyt had taken her on a quick tour of the grounds that first weekend, keeping all conversation to the compound. His sun-beaten face held the smile of a man who'd seen a lot in his lifetime. Only in the last days had he opened up to her a little. She learned he'd worked in Texas for years on ranches but didn't offer how he'd come to work at Agrarian Lodge. Martha had confided that he'd lost his wife a few years back and hadn't been the same since. She never elaborated, but the conversation left Kay feeling that the two of them had known each other before coming to lodge.

Chapter Three

Travis she knew; that was why she'd been invited and it was the main reason she went. After his joking offer of a job, followed by a contract, Kay wanted to see him in person. Their friendship had blossomed in a strange way. They met in the Hamptons a few summers before, discussing ginseng in prepared ice teas while standing in line at a deli. Outside, they'd continued their conversation when he mentioned he was heading to North Carolina to take a job at a new lodge on the coast. She'd offered she was battling her way through a two-year course at a prestigious cooking school, majoring in desserts and pastries. They'd become fast friends that day outside the deli.

They'd headed to the beach and shared a makeshift picnic while getting to know each other better. It was a relaxing day, the instant chemistry between them palpable. While Kay hadn't been promiscuous, her recent divorce and newfound freedom had given her courage to experiment with her handsome, motorcycle-riding new friend. Her divorce was mentioned in passing but not detailed for him. He admitted he didn't want commitments, only to enjoy his bachelor lifestyle. She understood, as her new focus was being true to herself and her own wants.

Placated from the food, wine, conversation, and setting, Travis asked a leading question, one she hadn't debated herself yet.

"What are you game for, Kadence? Tell me what you wanted your ex to do to you that you never asked for or he never did." His lips curled into a sly smile. "Look at us this way, for a few hours we can enjoy each other with abandon. No guilt, no repercussions, just lust."

Kay didn't have an answer. Her mind was lost—how to tell this sexy man that she wanted everything he would offer. That his touch would be so different from any other she'd ever felt. He continued staring at her, silently letting her know he understood her dilemma of conscience. She never felt fear of him, only anticipation she couldn't define. She was actually going to have sex with a stranger, just because she was horny. He was hot and different, the ultimate personification of the bad boy image. Yes, she decided she was. Whatever happened, she'd live with the consequences. Travis spoke while Kay silently debated her choices.

"I suppose if he touched you right, you might still be together. But then his loss is my reward." Travis reached for her hand, locking it in his as he gently directed her away from the beachfront, back to where he'd left the motorcycle. Kay figured he would take her to a hotel, and she was about to offer her hotel name when she realized he had other ideas.

* * * *

Their whirlwind weekend at the beach made her realize her life would continue, but with her in charge of her future. In the past, she would have shied away from any sexual contact with a stranger. That weekend, she'd abandoned all her long-held concepts of propriety. Her body heated as she remembered how her ride on his motorcycle had left her body humming. Holding tight to Travis's waist while they toured the back roads, it was at her instigation that they pulled over in a quiet, secluded area. While Travis was a willing participant, it was her idea to move forward and sit facing him, using the handlebars to lean back against. She'd started by stroking his hard cock through his jeans, taking his hand to her breast, pressing his fingers with hers to show him the power she needed to feel. It was definitely her idea to open his zipper and palm his cock. When she knew he was close to coming, she asked him to turn on the machine, tugging her short denim skirt up around her hips. Travis needed no further invitation, his large fingers stroking her pussy while his other hand pumped her breast. Her fingers moved the small swath of lace aside that covered her clit, moving his hand to bare skin. Travis had followed her lead, slipping his middle finger in her pussy. When he had her wet and needy, she asked if he had a condom. With little fuss, he pulled one from his wallet and handed it to her. Tearing the package open, she quickly sheathed his cock, pausing to stroke him several times. She made the decisive move to shift further and drop her pussy over his hard cock. With small movements, she took his cock deeper in her body, using the machine's motion to drive him deeper inside her.

Kay knew Travis was enjoying the moment, his groin riding against her clit as he continued to pump her breasts. For the first time in her life, she didn't care about being the proper woman; she cared about what her body was feeling, the need created within her. While the motorcycle continued to idle under them, their slow fuck built into a frenzy each time he'd hit the throttle. Kay had thrown her head back and rested her shoulders against the handlebars, her body spread wide for Travis's touch.

Their time on the motorcycle was one of Kay's most erotic memories, one she cherished for the absolute abandon. She'd come several times that afternoon, knew Travis had come twice, too. What could have been an awkward parting was filled with laughing and promises to keep in touch. She figured she'd never see him again. They stayed in contact through an occasional e-mail and phone call. While they had enjoyed their afternoon together, they both understood it wouldn't be a permanent relationship, both of them heading in different directions for career requirements.

Kay had accepted the experience for just that, a time in her life when she let social mores go and enjoyed the experience. Travis on his motorcycle was a hard act to follow, an experience she knew she'd never recapture, so it was best to let it go and enjoy the memory of complete abandon. She knew that very day their relationship wouldn't be permanent, rather a moment in time to savor.

There had been no nerves when she traveled to the Lodge for the job interview. If she and Travis fell into bed, it would be for mutual gratification, not with the idea of a long-term, all-encompassing relationship. They could have fun together, but she knew how important Travis's job was to him. If she took the position as pastry chef, their working together would be more important than a quick lay occasionally. But she still remembered the euphoria she felt when he brought her back to her car that night. Her body still tingled from the power of the machine they'd fucked on. When settled in her own vehicle, she had an odd feeling of accomplishment as she drove back to her hotel with Travis' touch still present on her body. She had a small orgasm on the drive home when her cum dripped from her body, making her squirm against the liquid.

That night at her hotel, lying naked on her bed, she'd used her own hand to squeeze her nipple while reliving the feel of Travis's cock in her body. Using her own fingers and eventually a dildo from her suitcase, she used the lubricant on her clit, wishing it was his cum making her slippery as she manipulated her clit and pussy while pushing the toy deep inside her, imagining it was his cock fucking her again. Kay was smart enough to know you could never relive a moment like that, but she'd cherish the memory of how her body hummed under his touch. It was a memory she'd often used to masturbate to, although she never truly achieved the level of fulfillment of that first time.

Her one regret was that she hadn't managed to change their positions and suck his cock. He was long and thick, stretching her body to accommodate his girth. She'd wanted to feel his cock in her ass, too, but they hadn't managed to complete that act, only his large finger sliding in and out of her anus while his cock fucked her pussy. No matter what, after her staid marriage, her moment in time had left her with hope for finding another man in the future who would play her body the way Travis had.

* * * *

There were sexual tensions between them when they met a second time at her interview for the job. Her visit to Agrarian Lodge had reinforced the concept that they'd be casual lovers. He'd taken her out for supper the night before she left and kissed her. The chemistry between them was deep and easy. Their playful touching in his car had led them to a nearby hotel for a few hours. Kay remembered they laughed easily as he tossed several condom packages on the bedside table while they tore at clothes, tossing them onto the floor.

He had large hands that molded to her form, teased her nipples, and pinched her ass. The intensity they touched and fucked with was pleasurable, and they'd both had fun. Travis was tall, over six feet, which melded well with her height. He licked her pussy to perfection, making her come with his fingers buried in her pussy as he sucked her clit. He had a long, thick cock that she enjoyed sucking. He had a very expressive face, letting her know with few words what pleasured him and how frustrated she made him, stalling his climax while she sucked him. She'd watched his expressions as she did and knew he'd come down her throat when she slid her moist index finger in his anus.

After that, they'd rested and shared several sodas from the vending machine while talking seriously about life, work, and the possibility of her taking the job with Travis as her boss. It was decided she wanted the job, but it wouldn't be wise for them to continue a flaming romance in full view of the staff. Travis had accepted her decision, but that didn't mean they couldn't enjoy the rest of their night.

They'd gone on to fuck with abandon, Travis taking her from behind at first, sliding his cock in and out of her body with smooth moves as his hands reached around and palmed her breasts. She'd ridden him in a reverse cowgirl, taking him deep in her pussy. He'd fingered her anus until she shuddered then turned her under him, taking her legs high on his shoulders while he penetrated her ass. He'd fucked her anus until she'd come a second time, finally letting himself come deep inside her. She smiled at the memory, knowing in a different situation, they would have had more fun for a while longer. But she knew directly from when they'd first met that he had a short attention span when it came to women. It was amicably decided they'd remain friends and find other people to have relationships with. Their best bet for a lasting relationship was as friends and business associates. She hadn't told him of her fantasies of having him and Stuart in her bed at the same time. That was another topic best left unspoken. For her, it was a valid want, one she would push to make happen.

* * * *

Travis stood, a large, six-foot, solid man. He had more tattoos than she'd seen to date and long graying hair that was always pulled back in a ponytail at the base of his neck. A bandana was always folded and knotted around his forehead. The motorcycle he drove finished his attitude. While he was quick to laugh, she knew he would also be quick to lash out if necessary. After their night of experimentation, she'd teased him, telling him that in the short time she'd been at Lodge, she knew they'd be just friends because he was secretly in lust with Lisa. At first, he'd laughed at her idea. But the longer she kept his gaze, the sooner he turned away, giving her the answer she knew was right. They only discussed Lisa once between them, and it was Travis's feelings that held him back. He'd explained to Kay he was an all-or-nothing kind of guy and Lisa wanted no part of him. So he'd been content to watch from the corners.

Kay had no words of reassurance for him, so instead she opted for silence. Travis appreciated her approach and had opened up more and more. He was becoming a trusted friend, one of the few who knew about the real reason for her divorce. Working together would be manageable. While their styles were different, her duties lay in a specialized area she liked, and he oversaw the rest of the kitchen and the staff.

The lodge itself had sold her on the job. The timber-frame structure was huge. It had ten master suites and slept twenty people. The living area on the main floor off the reception hall was large and roomy. A gigantic stone fireplace anchored the room where seating areas had been positioned. The dining room was behind it, the trestle table long enough to seat twenty guests easily. Behind the dining area was a library, tastefully decorated and designated as a smoking parlor, its walls lined with books on custom-made shelves. A second room was an open, den-like space, a large television centered on the main wall. In the far corner was a well-stocked bar. Most afternoons, drinks and snacks were served there before supper.

The compound had two separate guest homes, each able to sleep eight. These were usually occupied by smaller parties who wanted to have more privacy. Each home had a fully stocked kitchen. These were the only places where children were allowed to stay. No children under the age of sixteen were invited into the main lodge. The private homes only accepted children from twelve to sixteen. Travis had explained to her that Stuart understood the importance of bonding between parent and child, memories he'd never have himself, but it was lodge policy and not to be broken. At first Kay thought it was an elitist attitude, but after talking with Lisa one day, she realized it was more for safety than anything else. Apparently Mr. Drake didn't mind children, as long as they were well behaved and looked after. His insurance carriers liked it that way, too. Since the lodge offered hunting and fishing, as well as day trips in the area, most guests preferred it to be an adult experience.

There was a fifty-acre stocked pond on site as well as the waterfront that ran along the sheltered cove where Agrarian Lodge sat. With the Atlantic Ocean just a few minutes away by boat, the experience was awe-inducing the first time she'd been taken on a boat ride. Seeing the lodge from the water gave her a different perspective.

And that was what Stuart had wanted to create, an escape for adults. From Tuesday afternoon through Sunday afternoon, guests were treated like royalty. In the last months, most of their bookings had been groups looking for a specialized retreat. The corporate world had found them and was snapping up weeks as bonuses for its executives. Whatever Stuart had in mind to begin with, his dream must be close to coming true, Kay decided. He'd seen his vision go from dream to paper and from design to reality. So now he was an innkeeper, and apparently a very good one at that, which led her right back to him again. Stuart Drake would be trouble for her if she let him. The bigger unknown was if he'd be interested in her.

Chapter Four

The home improvement center was the last place Kay thought she'd run into Stuart Drake on a Thursday night. Her cart, one wheel deliberately going horizontal instead of vertical, was loaded with starter plants. She had small herbs and several varieties of tomatoes and cucumbers. She'd decided against trying to grow lettuce this first year, but couldn't resist the brightly colored petunias. There was also a bag of gladioli bulbs as well as some tulip bulbs, which she hoped would come up next spring. A sack of plant food was stashed under the basket and several rolls of bunny wire were perilously balanced on top of it. Folding her list and shoving it in her back pocket, she turned to see him watching her from across the aisle.

* * * *

Stuart stopped at the home center, hoping to gather some material on kitchen cabinets. While his new home was basically set, the drawings could still be changed at this stage. Deciding what the kitchen would look like was a big decision. Beyond the money involved, he wanted a working space that was efficient and comfortable. In the back of his mind, he'd always longed for what television had taught him was a normal family. Mom making a meal, the kids running in and out while Dad sat at the table reading his newspaper. Laughing to himself about the absurdity of his fantasy, he looked up and thought he saw Kay cross the building. He followed automatically, the all-important cabinets forgotten with just a glimpse of her. Staying in the background, he watched her select the plants and assorted items for her garden.

He should have turned and walked away, but he didn't. Guilt had gotten to him right after the meeting Wednesday. While she was simply asking to put in a small garden, he'd blown the situation into a grudge match. Knowing he didn't want the animosity between them, it was a good enough excuse to approach her in the garden center. Only now that she was this close to him, the words stuck in his throat.

Simple jeans and a sweater weren't meant to look that good on any woman. Her hair glinted in the fading daylight, red and gold highlights dancing against the dark brown strands. Tonight she'd left it down, falling around her shoulders. She was a large woman, he knew. Having seen her standing beside Travis, he knew she was only a few inches shorter. Her well-proportioned body intrigued him. She had an hourglass figure, all curves and grace. Her large breasts narrowed to a slim waist and smoothed to larger hips that melted into long, strong legs that he dreamed of wrapped around him. Stuart liked tall women, being six foot four inches himself—a smaller woman seemed dwarfed beside him. A woman like Kadence could hold her own standing next to him. His thoughts were exposed when he met her look. Neither of them moved for a long time, Stuart finally forcing his legs to work, bringing him beside her.

"Hi."

"Hi," she answered hesitantly. Holding his look for an intense moment, he was the first to look away, not missing her hold back a smile in his peripheral vision.

"You've got a good start here," he began, feeling like he was sixteen all over again.

"We'll see…" She was coaxing him, and he decided to play.

His dark eyes flashed back to hers, and he let himself laugh out loud. "I didn't mean to turn your garden into a guilt project. It's just that a lot of people start out strong and seem to fizzle halfway through a project."

"And I seem like a fizzler to you?" she asked, her one eyebrow cocked, her words low and smooth. His fingers automatically moved to his temples, massaging his head in times of stress. "What don't you like about me, Mr. Drake? Somehow I get the feeling I've annoyed you already, though I'm not sure how or why. Maybe we could get a cup of coffee and discuss it?"

He absorbed her words and knew she was right. He felt it, too—the tension between them was thick. Whether he was going to admit to it or not remained to be seen. He hadn't decided how to handle her yet.

"This is your day off. I don't want to intrude." Her outright laugh at his refusal wasn't what he expected. "And since we don't really know each other, you haven't annoyed me…yet!"

"But you're anticipating my being a thorn in your side. Why?" Kay glanced around the crowded aisle of the garden center. Stuart knew this wasn't the place to taunt each other, especially new boss and employee, but he was so close to her and didn't want the time to end. It had been a long time since he met someone to verbally spar with.

"Let's just say I hope you'll prove me wrong." His look caught hers, testing to see if she'd push him or let him go.

"I hope so, too, but it would be a lot easier if I knew what I was being measured against."

"Not measured, Ms. Farrell. We just don't know each other."

"Yet…" He felt his cheeks heat at her one-upping him. He wasn't sure if she could see his erection and dropped his hand holding the pamphlets to block her view. Kay laughed at him openly for the second time that night. "Why, Mr. Drake, you do blush so coyly."

"And you, Ms. Farrell, should know I don't tread on another man's territory." His harsh words matched his tone, and he turned to walk away. Only her hand on his upper arm kept him from making his escape.

"Wait, please." He hesitantly turned back to her, scanning the crowded area. "Why did you hire me if you thought I was romantically involved with Travis? That wouldn't be a wise business decision."

"Travis does a great job of running the kitchens. If having you work beside him will keep him happy, it's fine by me. Only, don't presume to play with us both." When he turned from her a second time, she let him go.

* * * *

His words spun through her mind for long minutes after he'd left her, her cart all but forgotten. The image swam before her eyes, her body sandwiched between this stoic man and his motorcycle-riding friend. She got a chill of anticipation and enjoyed the heat it created deep inside her pussy. Only when she was asked to move aside did she snap out of her self-imposed stupor. All the way home she debated his words. Obviously he thought she was sleeping with Travis. Now she had to find out whether it was because of something Travis had said or intimated or if it was Stuart's idea. Either way, it had to be dealt with as soon as possible.

* * * *

Two days later, she got a message from Lisa that Stuart wanted to see her when she had time. While she initially thought to corner him and have it out about her nonsexual relationship with Travis, she decided to wait and see how he handled her.

When the evening meal was well under way and her work completed, she slipped out of her white coat and glossed her lips. Last night, she'd gone back to the kitchen after supper and had a beer with Travis. She told him about her faux pas in the grocery store the night before, asking where the kosher aisle was for matzos. He'd laughed heartily over her northern assumption and then told her the names of several stores in Wilmington where she could find specialty items. It had broken the ice, and she'd asked him straight out if he'd told Stuart they were an item. His response seemed genuine that he hadn't, although he did add that something was odd with Stuart's behavior since she'd arrived.

Travis had gone on to insinuate that maybe the gruff bachelor had taken one look at her and finally fallen head over heels in love, with her. They'd both laughed at the idea, but secretly Kay wondered what it might be like to be loved by him. She'd excused herself for the night with too much on her mind.

So here she stood, just outside his private office after receiving his summons. Somehow she felt like a child being called to the principal's office. Standing to her full height, which was now two inches taller in the clogs she used as work shoes, she knocked with a loud thump on his wooden door. A muffled "In" was all she got, so she opened the door to his inner sanctuary. It was the first time she'd seen the space, and she wasn't surprised to find old Harley sprawled out on the leather sofa under the window. Stuart nodded to her and then to the empty chairs in front of his desk while he ended his telephone call.

* * * *

As soon as her head peeked around the door, he knew he'd lost all concentration. Watching her enter, size up his space, and walk to the dog wasn't what he expected. Most people would take the chair across from him and try to act like they weren't listening to his conversation. Kay moved past him and sat on the floor beside the sofa, Harley's large head under her hand. He watched the two of them for a second then finally hung up the phone. With her back to him, he openly surveyed her with his dog, who now rolled onto his back in a compete act of submission and was enjoying the rewards of his trust, a two-handed belly rub that had the dog's eyes rolling back in his head. His left hind leg started to move with her motion, and she was laughing openly at the dog, talking to him as if he were a person who could understand. The worst part was that Stuart often spoke to the dog in much the same way, using him as a sounding board to work through a problem or an idea. Never before had he wished he was his dog, but today, with Kay's hands rubbing him, he would have gratefully switched places. The idea made him shake his head, and he laughed aloud.

"What are you laughing at, Mr. Drake?" she asked, not moving from her place. With her back to him still, he watched, her hair still braided down her back.

"I was wondering what Harley was thinking right now." Knowing damn well he couldn't tell her his real thoughts, it was as close as he could get to the truth.

"And are you jealous of him, too?" He felt Kay had gone too far, but it was too late to pull back her snap comment. He decided she was right but blunt, something most of his employees refrained from. He'd been hoping to clear the air between them but assumed he'd control the conversation. Stuart shuffled papers on his desk, the movement an apparent stall for time and focus.

"Not jealous of Harley, Ms. Farrell, but definitely careful of my friends' feelings."

"Do you really think I took this job to be close to Travis, because it was a sexual thing as opposed to a work thing?"

"I think it was one option." There was no other explanation he could come up with. Why would a pastry chef from Manhattan choose to hide away in a small lodge in coastal Carolina? She was either running to something, Travis, or running away from something. Somehow she didn't seem the type to cut and run.

"And you don't mess with your best friend's girl, is that it?"

"Yes. All those unspoken rules we men live by." Holding back a groan, he realized this was one of those times his morals were being tested beyond his limits.

"I see." Finally, she moved slowly from the floor, her action not appreciated by Harley, who flopped back onto his belly and let out a yawn. She laughed at the dog and tousled his ears one last time before taking the chair across from Stuart's desk. "Lisa said you wanted to see me." She was all business before him now. The change in her persona was overwhelming.

"I'd like to apologize if I seemed hard on you about the garden. I've learned good intentions don't always work out and I was just trying to be…prepared."

"In case I didn't follow through, or in case you decided I didn't work out as expected and you let me go?"

"Both and neither." He let a smile slip and closed his eyes against the sight of her pouty lips. "All I'm saying is if it will make your time here more pleasant, plant the damn thing. I don't care about it…" Stuart pushed back in his chair and became engaged in the scene outside his window.

"What do you care about, then? Something has you all riled up, and apparently, it's me. Or my presence here. What do you want from me, Stuart?" This time she caught his look and held it, all but daring him to look away first. It was an old trick, Stuart knew, one she must have acquired from her courtroom days. No matter what, don't blink first. This time he played along, not letting her see him flinch at her words. For a long time they were silent, intent on playing out the trap they'd gotten themselves into. Only the slamming of a car door outside his window snapped his look from hers.

"The guests are back from their boat trip."

"Fine, that still doesn't answer my question."

Stuart thought about all the questions he wanted answers to but refrained from verbalizing any of them. Since she arrived at the lodge, he'd spent too many nights wondering all sorts of things about Kadence.

"The bill, from the garden center," he stated and cleared the frog from his throat. "Drop it by when you get a chance, and I'll reimburse you." He managed to work the conversation back to business. It was self-preservation on his part. He watched several things cross her face, none of which she shared with him. Only her dark eyes watching him intently let him know the bill was the last thing on her mind.

"Thanks, but no thanks. It's my hobby. I'll pick up the tab. Next year if we're both still here, we'll discuss you covering the expense. For right now, I'm more comfortable with it this way."

"But it's a legitimate business expense."

"I understand that, but I think I'll enjoy my hobby a lot more without the pressure."

"As you wish. If you change your mind, just get me the bill."

"I won't change my mind."

"Fine." Purely for a distraction, Stuart glanced at the papers on his desk.

"Am I dismissed?" she asked when it became apparent he'd shut down.

"What?" he said, hoping to make her think he'd forgotten about her, when in reality his erection was about to burst through the zipper on his jeans. "Oh, yes, that's all." He didn't raise his head to watch her walk away. He studied her form from under his lashes.

She left quietly with Harley following close at her heels. When she got to the door, she knelt down and took the dog's large head between her hands. Talking directly to him she said, "Better stay here or he'll get pissed at you too!"

He glanced up when he heard her words, and she gave him a pressed-on smile before leaving his office. When she had closed the door behind her, he started muttering under his breath. He cursed her, the dog, and the fates that had her meeting Travis in that deli so long ago. Feeling infinitely better than he had before, he refrained from watching Kay walk to her apartment. He didn't need to watch her—he'd memorized her walk.

* * * *

Kay walked to her apartment and slipped on a bathing suit. A few laps would unwind her before supper and hopefully cool her down. In the weeks she'd been at Agrarian Lodge, Stuart hadn't made an appearance at the pool. None she was aware of, anyway. Her swim while the guests enjoyed their evening meal usually gave her complete privacy. It was a luxury to have access to such a beautiful space. The glass-enclosed atrium extended from the back of the lodge, and at twilight, the illusion of being outdoors became overwhelming.

* * * *

Stuart sat at his desk, his head dropped back against the leather chair, his hand absently stroking Harley's head. After Kay left, he'd wandered over to Stuart and dropped his head on his leg, his large eyes sad-looking. "I know how you feel, old boy. At least she touches you." Stuart groaned and felt himself throb once again. Even after overhearing Kay and Travis in the kitchen last night, he still kept his reserve. If his thoughts of them being romantically involved were wrong, well, didn't that make his situation even worse? Knowing she was free and still unapproachable from a business standpoint just plain sucked from his perspective.

He gave the dog one last pat before wandering to the window, his thoughts lost when he saw a lone swimmer in the pool. It didn't take a genius to know it would be her. She'd taken to using the pool while the guests ate, and it was Stuart's bad luck that one side of his office overlooked the atrium. Forcing himself, he moved away, knowing watching her long limbs slice through the water would be worse in the long run. Already in his dreams she wrapped them around him, pulling him tighter to her. He visibly quaked at the idea of being buried inside her and let his mind wander over the possible ways of getting to that point. Always, his imagination let him spend copious amounts of time kissing her before moving to her breasts, breasts he longed to lavish with attention.

Chapter Five

Staff meals were an experience unto themselves. Martha was chief in her kitchen and made sure everyone knew it. While she gratefully accepted any baked goods Kadence offered, her menus weren't discussed or debated. All employees who resided on site knew the house rules. Breakfast was at six-thirty. If you missed it, that was your problem. Only the coffeepot was left on for stragglers. Lunch was always something cold and prepared in advance. Supper was at seven, and again, if you were late, you missed it.

Meals were served family style around the large kitchen table. Conversation ran from the weather to world news to the guests' peculiarities. And always, someone had the bad sense to mention religion or politics before the meal ended, usually with Martha shooing everyone from her domain.

The staff enjoyed the main floor of the women's residence as a communal living area for television and card games. It was rumored that no man had set foot on the steps to the second story since Martha came to Lodge. By midnight, everyone was expected to be turned in for the night, whatever that meant to each of them, as long as the downstairs was quiet and empty. Martha accomplished this quite efficiently by having her bedroom on the main floor, where even a creaky floorboard garnered her attention.

It seemed like a good pattern, and most of the employees seemed reasonably content with their positions, petty personal problems aside. It was also widely known that Mr. Drake felt all his employees were treated quite well, and if someone didn't think so, they were free to move on and find other work and accommodations. So far, none had left for that reason.

* * * *

Kay found herself sitting on an overturned plastic bucket later that night, the dogs all pushing for her attention. She petted each one in turn and fed them only bits of the dry dog food they were normally given. While she had some bones left over from beef stock, she'd frozen them, hoping to be able to offer them to Harley one day as a treat. But since Stuart had come back from his trip, she'd seen little of the old dog, unless Stuart was nearby.

Holding the collar of one of the beagles, she turned it to check his name, calling the dog by it and trying to commit it to memory. Each one had his or her own personality, she was learning, and their names seemed to match.

Tulula was an attention hound, while Belle was quiet and restrained until called by name. Zoe was sweet, with hound dog eyes that made Kay want to give her an extra morsel of treat. Roger was a bully, pushing the rest out of the way for his share of attention. Tex had an attitude, and Rocky had a dark patch of fur around his left eye, making him look like he just left the boxing ring and wasn't the winner. Mavis was sweet and reserved, just short of skittish.

Chloe, on the other hand, was sick, Kay decided. Something about her wasn't right, but she couldn't put her finger on what was wrong. The dog took her offered treat and accepted the attention given her, but her eyes were dull, not like the young dog she'd met a few weeks ago. When her pocket was empty of the kibble, she gave them each one last pet and stood, brushing off the back of her jeans. Only when she turned to leave the pen did she realize she wasn't alone.

Stuart stood in the shadows watching her. Hesitating for only a few seconds, she spoke before she could change her mind. And she had to do something—the way he was looking at her made her uncomfortable in a way she'd long ago lost. He was leaning against the far post, his back resting against it, one long leg planted firmly on the ground, the other bent at the knee, resting on the same post. His arms were folded across his stomach, his hat pulled down, blocking his eyes. "There's something wrong with Chloe."

* * * *

"You went ahead and grew up, didn't you, girl. I missed it, but the boys didn't." He glanced to Kay before giving the dog one last pat and setting her down.

"I think our young girl is soon to be a mother," Stuart offered, holding the pen gate for her to slip out. Kay was still startled that the rest of the pack didn't launch themselves toward her, trying to get out.

"She's pregnant?"

"I think so," he said back, locking the gate behind him. "She's a little young. We were waiting for her first heat to have her fixed. I can only assume we missed it."

"Will you keep the puppies?" Stuart tried to focus on the dog, but his mind had her reaching up to touch his cock.

"Let's make sure that's her problem first. I'll call the vet in the morning, see if he can drop by. Then we'll worry about the puppies."

"I'm glad it's nothing serious. Two nights ago she seemed strange, but two nights before that she seemed fine." Kadence was walking beside Stuart toward the main road. Their conversation was easy, considering their past confrontations.

"You like dogs? You memorized all their names already."

"Yes, we always had several around the house when I was growing up. My mom was a teacher, and somehow everybody knew if you found a dog and couldn't keep it, Mrs. Farrell would help you find a home for it. Only sometimes the home she found was ours."

Stuart decided her smile would be his complete downfall if he wasn't careful. And he'd begun to see how Travis had become so entranced by her.

"Did your father see that as a problem?" He was thankful his voice hadn't cracked when he spoke, searching for a neutral conversation as opposed to spilling out his real thoughts. Although, he was intrigued by the idea of what her reaction would be. If he confessed his lust for her, he knew the odds were against him in all directions. First, it would hurt Travis, and second, he didn't want her to know she affected him. Sharing his weakness toward her, he'd lose all advantage as the boss and a man.

"He'd grumble and complain about the hair on his good jacket, but when my mother finally found a home, he'd be the first one in tears when the dog left with its new owner. And a few he never let be adopted." Kay hesitated a moment and then shared the rest of her thought. "Of course, if you ever met him, he'd say Mom and her dogs ate him out of house and home and made him put in an extra five years before his retirement."

Her laugh warmed him, and he pushed his hands in his back pockets to quell the urge to pull her to him. An urge he would have to come to terms with, for it was becoming harder to control the impulse.

"Was that really how it was?"

"To a point. He worked the extra five years because my mom wanted to put in her twenty-five before retiring. As for the dogs, they only have two now. That's the maximum the retirement community's bylaws will allow."

"So he's a softie deep down?"

"About the dogs, yes, and most things. Just don't piss him off. Then all hell breaks loose." Her smile gave way to a hint of the beautiful, yet rebellious child she might have been.

"Give me an example."

"Hurting any animal would trigger that response. Finding out I dented his car when I first got my license was a big deal." She laughed out loud, adding, "It was my own fault. I should have just told him to start with. It would have been much less painful." He glanced at her with his eyebrows furrowed, and she laughed again.

"Oh, no. He was terribly disappointed with me. His silent treatment was worse than any spanking would have been. And I wasn't allowed to use his car, ever again."

"Which hurt more, losing car privileges or his silent act?"

"Definitely the silence. I'd wait for him to come home to tell him about something good in my day or show him a test. He'd nod and open his newspaper." Kay hesitated but finally added, "I learned a lot that month about human nature and disappointment."

"Did your parents ever spank you?" he asked, liking the instant visual the idea provoked in his mind. And somehow, since he'd known her, he'd been close to wanting to take her over his knee. Never before had a woman pushed his buttons without really trying. Maybe that was her charm, but he wanted a physical release when it came to Kay. A kiss would be a start, one he knew would lead them into dangerous territory.

"No, I was never punished with physical means. My dad knew letting me know how disappointed he was in me was far worse. Let's just say I often wondered if the momentary pain of a spanking wouldn't have been better, at least when I was a kid. Even then, his quiet disdain was harder to bear."

"What finally broke the standoff?"

"My mother's birthday. She told us the only gift she wanted was her husband and daughter laughing together again. He finally brokered a truce…conversation, as if nothing had happened…but I never even considered asking to borrow his car again. Instead, I got a part-time job and saved up until I had enough to cover the repair cost."

"Did he take your money?" Stuart asked.

"Yes. After that, I kept the job and started saving for an old clunker to drive. When I found one, he upgraded me into a better car, but just by the amount of the repair bill." She was laughing, and Stuart wanted to drop his arm around her shoulder and pull her closer to him. He wanted to feel her against him. "Sometimes I still wish I'd never sold that old tin can."

"What about the other car you hit?"

"There wasn't any. I crushed the fender on a telephone pole that was at the exact corner of our driveway. I'll never know who decided the pole had to go exactly there, but it was a bitch of a turn if you didn't swing just right." Stuart laughed openly and watched her face as he did. She acted as if he never laughed. "Why, Stuart Drake, that's the first time I've ever seen you smile, let alone laugh out loud. You are human at times!"

Throwing back her head, she laughed with abandon. He still wasn't sure how this had all turned back onto him. Of course he smiled and laughed, sometimes. It was then he realized lately he hadn't. Changing the focus of their conversation back to her, he said, "He sounds like a good man."

"Within reason I'd say he was in most ways. I'm sure my mother would answer you differently, but her relationship with him was spousal, so her perspective is different. What about you, did your parents let you keep pets?"

Stuart's posture tightened for a few moments before relaxing.

"My mother didn't care as long as she wasn't responsible for it. My father died when I was very young. He was in the service, an accident on the training field."

"I'm sorry. It must have been difficult for you both."

The memory of him losing his father at a young age made him incredibly sad, especially after Kay shared the fender episode with him. The hardened tone of his response made him pause.

"I learned early on about being responsible for myself and for others, Kadence. I know firsthand that well-meaning intentions are just that, and until carried to term, just lip service most of the time."

She stopped walking and it took him several paces to realize he was alone. When he stopped and turned, she was staring at him, her mouth just short of hanging open. Unfortunately, the position left her lips in a soft oval, and Stuart didn't fight back the urge. All this time he'd wanted to touch her, and now he finally let himself have his moment.

In a few long strides he was back beside her, his hands on her shoulders. Staring at him, she didn't move when he dropped his head toward her, letting his lips brush against hers. His fingers tightened on her arms, and he deepened the kiss, letting the tip of his tongue taste the corners of her mouth before slipping between hers to find her heat. Kay wanted the kiss, he decided, as she slid against his body. He needed to know if there was something to the pull he felt for her or if it was just circumstance.

Her hand moved to his chest but didn't push him away. Instead, she stroked his chest until she felt the rhythm of his heart under her palm. He knew it speeded up at her touch and wondered if she could tell the difference. She shifted and opened her lips for him. The groan he let out worked its way up his chest long before he pulled back, his eyes searching hers.

"You were hoping it was just that I was forbidden to you, that one kiss and you'd be able to dismiss me. Only we both know that's not true, especially now."

"It doesn't mean I have to act on it. You're…"

"I'm my own person, and I make my own decisions. And I'm not romantically or sexually involved with Travis. We've been there, done that, and I accept that his attention span is too short for my liking. We've worked it out between us. Case closed. You have to decide where this goes."

* * * *

Kay took a deep breath and slowly moved away. The sun had set fully, and the mosquitoes were out in full force. Heading to her apartment, she spent the rest of her evening remembering and reliving his lips to hers. Standing before the bureau mirror brushing her hair, she remembered his body close to her and how she heated inside like never before. Her hand dropped to her crotch and lightly stroked against it. Her body shuddered, and she paused to enjoy the feeling.

"Damn him," she said to the reflection in the mirror. "It wasn't supposed to be like this. It's my turn to find a life, my time to explore for myself. Stuart Drake, I don't need the hassle!" The woman staring back at her started to laugh at the idea that she could control love or lust where Stuart was concerned. Being honest with herself, she finally admitted that she had taken the job to a certain extent because it would put her closer to him. That one lousy photograph had changed the track of her new life. Whether it was good or bad still remained to be seen.

When she stripped for her shower, she spent a few minutes pinching her nipples to hardness, watching them bud in the mirror. What she really wanted to feel was Stuart's lips to her breast, to feel how his short beard would tease her skin. She stood naked in her bathroom, imagining it was Stuart's hand cupping her breast while pinching her nipple. Using her other hand, she fingered her pussy to get the required response from her body. She had a small orgasm but nothing earth-shattering. Using a soft cloth against her clit under the flow of the hot water, she fantasized he was dropped to his knees before her, licking her clit until she came.

Lying in bed that night, she used both her toys to fuck her body, imagining it was Stuart's hands and cock filling her pussy and ass. Kay knew she had to get past the fantasy. The job meant a lot to her, and being lovesick over a man who obviously disliked her wasn't productive. But a girl could dream, as long as she remembered it was just a fantasy.

Chapter Six

It had been days since she'd seen him in person. Stuart had been a no-show in the kitchen since their kiss. She'd heard his voice in the main lodge several times, but he'd opted out of meals with the staff. This morning, Martha had mentioned it to her in passing.

"Don't know what bug got under his skin the last few days, but I hope it goes away soon. I've never known him to be so ornery."

"I find that hard to believe," Kay had automatically answered, and then wished she hadn't. Martha held her gaze for a second longer than necessary but didn't comment. Instead, they talked about the planned meals for the next few days as if her words hadn't been spoken.

Later that night she was in the main kitchen ladling strawberry preserves into clean glass jars when Stuart stopped by. His words were terse as well as his attitude.

* * * *

Stuart stayed in the hallway, half listening to her telephone call, half trying to pull himself away. He'd answered the call on the Lodge's main line and immediately didn't like the man's tone. His attitude annoyed him. While the caller never stepped over to rude, Stuart felt he was being handled.

"Put me through to Katie Farrell. This is her husband calling long distance, and I'm in no mood to hold."

The statement left Stuart cold. He'd remained professional but curt. He was more surprised when he called over to Martha and found out Kay was working in the kitchen tonight. He just assumed the place would be empty and shut down for the night. He was instantly glad he hadn't known she was there, for he knew he'd have made an excuse to visit her. He could have transferred the call but chose to walk across the lodge and catch a glimpse of her.

"There's a call for you, line three." He'd all but barked out the words at her, startling her, probably because she thought she was alone.

Even though he was the owner, he knew it was tacky to be hiding in the hallway listening to her half of the conversation. Yet here he was, afraid of being caught but not afraid enough to move on. He dismissed leaving and leaned on the hallway wall, openly listening to both sides of their conversation. Stuart immediately blessed speaker phones.

* * * *

Kay was instantly on alert. Anyone who called her this late in the evening would use her cell. She grabbed a dish towel and wiped her hands on the way to the wall-mounted unit beside her work area, pausing to hit the speaker button before talking.

"Kadence Farrell." The adrenaline was pumping through her veins, and she hoped this wasn't going to be a disaster.

"Hello, Katie, my dear. Miss me?"

Kay didn't hold back the groan that her throat emitted. The adrenaline stopped dead in her system, and now she only felt tired. She took a quick glance around her work space. The job she was enjoying was suddenly turned to drudgery, but she knew she had to keep going. "Hello, Eric. What do you want?"

"Not a good attitude, Katie, especially when I've been left in limbo for so long. I was just about to hang up, and you know how it annoys me to have to call back."

"Don't call me Katie, and why are you calling?"

Eric wasn't prepared for her attitude.

"I'm just checking on you, my sweet. Is your little baking job as satisfying as you thought, or are you just sticking it out because you don't want to come crawling back?"

"Considering we've been divorced for over two years and separated another before that, what makes you think I'd come crawling back to you? And just for the record, my little baking job is going fine. I like the lodge, its surroundings, and especially its people."

"Oh, yes, your motorcycle fling, Taylor or Tyler, isn't it?"

"Eric, you know very well his name is Travis, and we've had no fling. He's just a friend, and you still haven't answered my question. What do you want?"

"I was serious. I want to know if you're ready to come home."

Laughing outright at him probably wasn't Eric's first desired response, Kay decided, knowing how surprised he would be by her tone. But she remembered each reason for being so cold.

"Eric, we don't have a home for me to return to. All of that was dissolved years ago. I'm no longer your wife, your responsibility, or even your friend." She paused to push back the annoyance she was feeling, not wanting to give Eric the satisfaction of knowing he riled her. "What would Diana have to say about that? And how is Dee Dee doing? She must be walking and talking up a storm by now." Kay was wandering around the kitchen making a fresh pot of coffee while they talked. The long silence that ensued didn't bode well for anybody. "Eric, I asked how Dee is doing. Is she okay?"

"I assume so. I haven't seen her this week. Diana has moved out."

"Oh." While it wasn't the best reply, it was all she could think of at the moment with so much going through her mind.

Her marriage had finally dissolved when she learned of Diana's existence in Eric's life. The final blow was when she found out his mistress was carrying his child, something he'd all but forbidden her to do until they were better established in their careers and lives. But she tried to be fair and knew that she'd gone along with the decision at the time, willingly. Hell, she figured what's a year or two when you have a lifetime ahead.

"Oh! That's all you have to say? I expected more from you, Katie. You're an educated woman, and I expected a better response."

"Don't cop an attitude. You called me. Since you did, you obviously want to fill me in on the missing pieces, so go ahead. How did you screw up this marriage?" She found the simple rhythm of filling the jars was therapeutic as she listened to her ex-husband.

"I didn't." Anger filled the room with his booming voice. A sick chill ran through her when she heard this tone in his voice, instantly remembering the other times she'd been the recipient of this attitude. Kay took a breath and remembered she wasn't married to him and didn't have to absorb his anger.

"Eric, really. In any relationship there are two points of view." Kay didn't spur him on. A protracted silence enveloped them all.

"Dee may not be mine. Until the paternity test comes back next week, we decided some time apart was best."

Kay's first reaction was to say, "Oh" again. She fought the urge and found herself saying instead, "I'm sorry, Eric. This must put all of you in a difficult position."

"Not difficult. If she's not mine, I want nothing to do with her ever again. If she is, I'll pay." His words halted before he added, "And pay and pay."

"It all boils down to the money with you. If she's your child, she deserves more than a check once a month. You owe it to her to spend time with her and…"

"Oh, Katie, cut the dramatics. We both know I never wanted her. Actually, I'm hoping it turns out in my favor. I could be rid of both of them much easier that way."

"You're a bastard, Eric. I'm still not sure how I was so blinded by you for such a long time."

"Not blinded, baby. You know I'll always love you. You never gave us a chance to work through our problems."

"No. I don't accept that. You had an affair. I didn't. And when I asked you to go to counseling, what happened? You went to the first two appointments and then found you were too busy. Unfortunately, we both know what you were busy doing while I was in therapy trying to save our marriage."

"I was only banging her, baby. You I made love to."

Kay caught a glimpse of Stuart moving from the shadows in the doorway, his hands balled into fists, apparently livid at Eric's remark, but she didn't let on she'd seen him. But now she knew he'd been listening to her conversation. It circled around her mind that he could be trying to get to know more about her, or maybe he was just nosy. Either way, she'd explore those possibilities later. For now, she had to assert herself with her ex-husband and let Stuart know she wouldn't play games with any man when it came to their private lives. She wondered what Stuart's thoughts on her ex would be. Would he consider him a bastard, or was she just a woman who couldn't keep her man happy?

"Bite me, Eric. You cheated on both of us. You told her we were separated and I wouldn't let go. You told me you wouldn't see her again if I gave you a second chance."

"She was just a body, a piece of ass to pass an occasional afternoon."

"No, she was your mistress. Our divorce would have happened even if she was a one-night stand."

"None of it matters. I found out she was cheating on me, and now I see the light at the end of the tunnel."

"I'll bet you do. Have you had one of your law partners make up all the papers already? Cut them both out of your life completely? I find it amazing you have the balls to feel so violated and betrayed by Diana when you were doing the exact same thing to me."

"You were my wife…"

"And I'm not anymore. Good for me." She drew a deep breath and continued. "I've moved on, Eric. You should, too. I'd prefer it if you didn't call me anymore, especially on the business phone. If you have an emergency, please use my cell from now on. And before you say anything more, I really can't imagine what emergency you'd have to inform me about anyway."

"Some of our old friends still ask about you. They miss you."

"My old friends are still my current friends. Your friends are still yours. The only reason they were polite to me was because of you and your father."

"That's not true—don't you remember all those wonderful evenings at our home, with all of us laughing and sharing a meal? Come on, Katie, you remember." His voice turned smooth, and Kay pictured a snake-like creature holding the other end of the telephone, a striped tie wrapped around its neck.

"I remember entertaining your friends. I remember doing all the work and getting a pat on the head at the end of the night for a job well done. I remember you calling at two in the afternoon and telling me you'd invited ten people home for supper, not caring that I'd be in court all afternoon. I remember you assuming it was my responsibility. And I remember hating most of the people we entertained."

"No, you didn't. You enjoyed it as much as I did."

"No, I didn't. It was a lot of work and always on your terms. I enjoyed entertaining when I chose to, on a weekend with my friends."

"Please, don't remind me. How many weekends did I give up to your friends and their mundane life stories? Did you really think sitting around in jeans and sneakers, eating pasta, and drinking cheap wine was my idea of a fun Saturday night? Get real, Katie."

"I know it wasn't, and you were always so clever to let us know you thought us a waste of your precious time. And we never drank cheap wine, Eric. Your ego wouldn't allow it."

"Send me your contract. I'll find a loophole to get you out of it."

"*No*. I'm quite happy here. I like my job, and I'm not going to give it up for you or anybody else. If I wanted out, I'd exercise the back door I had written in." Kay sipped her coffee and organized her thoughts. Letting Eric get her all riled up wasn't acceptable anymore. "We're divorced, Eric. I have a new life. You need to get one too."

"Katie…"

"Eric, please don't call or contact me again. There's no real reason. I'll consider it harassment if you call back."

"Don't go all legal on me, Kadence."

"Why not, afraid I'll best you, again?" Her laugh rang through the kitchen, and she felt better immediately. Stuart wouldn't know the details of what she referred to, but it was enough for him to know she pissed off her ex.

"That was uncalled for," he told her in an indignant tone.

"I know, but it felt great. Get a life, Eric, don't call me again." She disconnected the speaker phone and poured herself a second cup of coffee. Only then did she allow herself the time to think about his words. Finally she let herself laugh out loud. There was justice in the world, sometimes you just had to wait for it to come full circle.

She was filling the jars again, her motions timed to the background music playing from the radio across the room. She'd started out with a classical station but found her mood lightened after Eric's call. Switching to classic rock and roll, her hips swayed with the notes as her canning continued. She knew from the shadows in the hallway Stuart had left but she also knew at some point he'd ask about her conversation, or at least, her relationship with her ex.

Kay wondered if he'd come back to the kitchen tonight or if he'd run back to this office.

Chapter Seven

An hour later Stuart couldn't keep himself from going back to the kitchen. He knew she was still working. All the lights reflected into the dark dining room hall when he left his office. He'd spent the time going over the conversation he'd eavesdropped on. It was enlightening to say the least. Her file had told him she'd been a public defender in Manhattan before going back to school. It was part of why he couldn't get a grip on her. Why would someone spend so much time and effort to get a law degree and then chuck it and become a pastry chef? While it didn't make sense to him, somehow he liked that she stood up for herself. It also made him realize he was dealing with a woman who stood her ground, not the fluff he'd originally thought to meet.

Watching her from the doorway, he cleared his throat to get her attention before walking to the coffeepot and pouring himself a cup. Old Harley followed at his heels.

"Everything okay at home? Your husband sounded upset when he called."

"My ex-husband, and I've asked him not to call me here again."

"It's not a problem, as long as it doesn't become a habit." Leaning against the counter at the far end of the room, he wondered how much information she'd offer.

"I'm sure you'd rather keep your lines clear for lodge business." End of subject. She wasn't going to talk to him about her conversation. Instead, she changed the dynamic of the situation.

"There's some fresh sourdough rolls in the pantry if you want to sample the preserves."

He put his cup aside and retrieved the baked goods, finding them still warm from the oven. Kay spooned some of the preserves into a small dish and placed it on the counter near him. Tearing open the roll, he dipped it in the sweet strawberry concoction and washed it down with a sip of coffee.

"Pretty good, but why are you canning at eleven o'clock at night?"

"Is it a problem?" She glanced from her jars to him and he shook his head. "Sometimes I like the quiet of the kitchen. I can think and work at the same time. Today I just felt like it."

"I'm just surprised you're not out with Travis tonight. Sunday night, tomorrow off, I figured you two would have plans."

"Travis had plans, and I did, too. His were to go into Wilmington and bar hop. Mine were to turn these bushels of strawberries into something other than compost." They were quiet while she finished the process. Kay poured a fresh cup of coffee. She brought to the table a metal tin of butter cookies, motioning for him to take a seat.

"Travis never had cookies or cakes around for us to snack on. Are you trying to make me fat?" he teased.

"Somehow I don't think a few pounds would hurt you either way."

"Brunch went well today, considering you were a person short."

She only glanced at him through her lashes before smiling. "Not much gets by you."

"Not much should. How will you handle your no-show?" He bit into a second cookie and savored the buttery texture. He decided Kay was holding back the smile that he noticed always found its way forward when someone enjoyed her labors of love. She took a cookie for herself and broke it into two pieces, savoring the taste before answering him.

"I'm not going to. When Travis does the payroll this week, he'll have to deal with him. It's better this way, until I get to know the staff a bit better. I don't know if this is a first-time absence or a habitual problem."

"You're right, let Travis handle it. But brunch went well. I got several positive comments as the group was leaving."

"That's nice to hear, thank you." She finished her cookie and pushed back in her chair, lifting her legs to the empty one beside her. Stuart watched her silently before breaking the standoff. What he wanted to ask her was why in God's name had she married such a stiff-ass jerk, but he knew he wouldn't. Maybe someday, but not now. Just the idea that he was picturing glimpses of the future with her was unsettling. Changing direction, he moved to a neutral topic.

"Chloe is pregnant." Stuart watched Kay's face light with relief.

"I'm glad she's not sick."

"So am I, but I'm not sure a full litter is what we need right now."

"I'll help with the pups," she offered.

His gaze flew to hers, holding for a second too long before he retreated to his coffee mug. Again there was a protracted silence between them. This time she just sipped from her cup and waited for him. After he had kissed her, she'd told him it was up to him if he wanted to continue or start, rather, a relationship. Somehow he didn't like the lawyerly vibe she was giving off, and he knew she realized why he'd come to talk to her. It was the proverbial kiss-off she'd been expecting. Having thought through the situation, he knew starting a relationship with her would not be productive for his business or his ego. How he handled her would be the interesting part. All of his preconceived statements fled his mind. He realized in that second he did want a relationship with her but knew he'd tell her different.

"Kadence, I'm sorry about kissing you the other night. I was out of line. As your employer, I don't want you to feel uncomfortable. It won't happen again, I promise."

"And what if I wanted it to?"

Suddenly confident, she baited him, he decided, purely for fun. She'd been prepared for him to back off, probably assumed it would be his play. Would she bust his balls for trying to do the right thing?

After the phone call he'd listened to earlier tonight, he'd decided if the roles were reversed, he'd probably bust her chops just for general principles, or an outlet for his angst.

"Doesn't matter. It can't be." He finally looked at her, waiting for her to acknowledge his words.

"All right, no problem."

Earlier he'd decided if she didn't want to pursue a relationship with him, he'd accept her decision with grace. The only alternative would surely make them both uncomfortable, and after all, it was just a kiss. An amazing kiss from his perspective, considering its length, but still just a kiss. His cock stirred, remembering the instant feelings his body felt during the kiss. "Fine, I should go." His tone sounded curt to his own ear, and he tried to change his tone. "I…"

"Leave this. I'll straighten up before I turn in." Stuart hesitated a second too long, and he watched her expression change, ultimately deciding to speak her mind. "Was I supposed to rant and rave and tell you I couldn't live without you fulfilling me as a woman?" She teased him openly, and while he understood it was a defense mechanism, he also knew deep down it wouldn't have bothered him if she'd given him just a little bit of a fight.

"Good night, Kadence. Thank you for making the preserves."

"You're welcome, Stuart. Good night."

He left quickly without another word. Harley slowly stood from his position in the doorway. For long seconds he looked after Stuart and back to Kay.

"Oh, go ahead, you old hound. Follow your master." The dog dropped his head and wandered slowly down the hallway.

* * * *

The cleanup went quickly, considering all that still had to be done. Even the repetitive tasks didn't soothe her tonight. Instead, she was keyed up and Stuart Drake was the reason. When he'd first come into the kitchen she wasn't sure what to expect. Stuart telling her she was hands-off was a possibility. Maybe it was for the best. Working relationships never worked out. But deep inside, she wondered what it might have been like between them. It was hard not to wonder how he would have reacted if she'd just walked over to him and dropped onto his lap. She imagined wrapping her arms around his shoulders and pressing her breasts against her chest. Her palm itched with a want to feel his cock, to learn the texture of his skin, his length and girth.

Looking at her reflection in the window over the kitchen sink, she said, "Back to the toys tonight," laughing at the absurd notion he'd been sexually interested in her.

Chapter Eight

Hearing the horse from behind gave her time to take a few cleansing breaths as she slowed her running pace. When the rider approached, he expertly maneuvered the large beast to within a foot of her, walking the animal beside her.

"Stuart, how are you?" she asked.

"Fine, Kadence, and you?"

"Fine." She followed the path toward the staff quarters, and he continued beside her. "What can I do for you?"

"I was wondering if I could pick your brain for a few minutes."

"Depends on how deep and what the topic is. What's on your mind?" For an instant, she gazed at him with a twinkle in her eye. Was she fantasizing he'd come to tell her he made a mistake and wanted to explore a relationship with her? He dismissed it quickly, reminding himself Stuart Drake didn't change his mind often.

Stuart knew what was on his mind, but verbalizing it was not his goal, although if he didn't keep a tight check on himself, he was bound to do just that. She had her hair pulled back in a long tail and a baseball-style cap shielded her eyes. He didn't stop himself from watching how she moved. Smooth and graceful, he acknowledged. That was what he liked about her. Even for her size, she seemed to float almost. He groaned aloud at his thought, and she glanced up at him. If she'd just started her run, it would have been better timing, he decided. Now she was soaked with sweat, the moisture molding her damp T-shirt to her curves. The stretch pants she had on left nothing to his imagination in regard to her strong thighs and long legs. Even in sneakers, she stood a sleek line.

"Stuart?"

"Yeah, ah, has anybody mentioned that I'm building my private residence, or am about to start?"

"Yes, it's been mentioned, and I've assumed the north corner of the property is the site. It's the only one cleared."

"Yes, well. I noticed the other night that you seemed to be hunched over at the counters. Are they uncomfortable for you to work at?"

"You get used to it, I guess." She stopped to retie her shoelace and continued after she was finished. She paused as if she'd lost her train of thought, glancing up at him, her hat shielding her eyes and most of her face. Being so high up on horseback, it all seemed a little surreal to him. Finally, she spoke. "You're what, six two or three?"

"Six four," he corrected.

She began walking again and the horse seemed to follow along at her pace effortlessly.

"I'm five ten. Most kitchens are designed for the average person, five four to five ten. That's why the thirty-six inch height. If I ever have a home and get to design the kitchen, I'll make mine four inches higher. I usually wear clogs when I'm cooking, so an extra inch or two would help. It wouldn't be great for your resale value, although I don't think you're building with the idea of selling anytime soon."

"The architect wants some final decisions about the layout and cabinetry, and I'm stalling him. I'm not sure what direction to go."

"You should ask Travis." Her gaze met his as she looked up to him and he smiled.

"I have. He said basically the same thing as you. Raise the base cabinets four to six inches and ask Kadence for her opinion." This time he laughed out loud.

"Great minds thinking alike and all that."

"Kadence, why did you give up your legal career? Even if you were divorcing your husband, I can't imagine going through all that schooling and walking away."

She stopped short, and even the horse was confused. Tugging the cap off her head, she pulled the elastic band from her hair and ran her hand through it. He steeled himself for some horrible reason.

"I gave up my legal career because I didn't like it. I still have a sincere appreciation for the law, when it's handled properly. I still believe in everyone's fundamental rights. For me the problem was more of pushing paper than helping mankind."

"That's not a full answer. You could have left the public defender's office, gone with an established firm, or started your own. Surely there had to be other aspects of the law that you were drawn to?"

"I was always drawn to the idealism of the law. The reality of it generally sucks."

"So you were disillusioned?"

"Basically." She hesitated, and he knew she was deciding what to tell him. Would she open up to him or shut down and push him away? She let out a heavy breath. "I always wanted to be a chef."

"Then why law school? I don't understand you at all."

"That's a two-way street, Mr. Drake. Why don't we start with you?"

"I'm a closed book, Kay. A baseball pitcher with a blown shoulder isn't worth much to any team. After that, I got lucky in the computer market. I got luckier selling out when I did. The profits allowed me to buy this land and build the lodge."

"All right, why the lodge?"

"That, my dear woman, would take much too long to answer." Silently, he added, *And it would tell you too much about my personal life.* More than he was comfortable sharing.

"Is it that you just don't want to answer at all, or is it only to me?"

"Why is it we always seem to wind up challenging one another?"

"I think it's chemical, Stu." She waited for an explosion at the shortening of his name but didn't get one. Instead, she got his standard answer.

"My name is Stuart, and I don't answer to Stu or any other form of it. Understood?"

"Understood," she told him, biting back a smile.

"Kind of like how you must feel when your husband calls you Katie?" This time he kept her look, taunting her with his words.

"How did you know he called me Katie?"

"That's how he asked for you on the phone," he told her quickly, hoping to cover his stupid slip.

"Katie bothers me because of the way he uses it, not necessarily the name itself. Besides, why my parents decided to name me Kadence is still a mystery to us all. Neither of my parents have any musical talent or military training. My father always said Mom liked the way it sounded, Kadence Farrell, and he decided it was easier to go along with her than to fight since he didn't have a better suggestion to fight for."

"You love them deeply, don't you? And you respect them as people, too," he added.

"Yes, I got lucky. I was blessed with hardworking, reasonably normal parents who wanted the best out of life for themselves and me and not necessarily just monetarily. I was taught to see the good in the small things in life."

"I envy you that, Kay. My mother wasn't a strong woman. When my father died, she just dissolved. If I'd been any younger, my life would probably have been very different."

"How old were you when he died?"

"Just turned seven. Old enough to take it to heart when people told me I was the new man of the house, and young enough to be scared to hell by the prospect of it all."

"And that's why you never married, afraid something similar would happen to your children?" They'd reached the garage building, and Stuart knew she'd leave him soon.

"That's another long story, too long for standing here when the mosquitoes are about to descend on us."

Kadence held his gaze for a long time before answering him. "For another time, then." Her hand reached slowly toward the beast Stuart straddled, hesitant yet determined. At first he thought she was reaching to him, then realized in time she was going to stroke the horse. He pushed back the realization of how close he'd been to reaching down and taking her hand. Instead, he watched her eyes widen as her fingers made contact with the horse's side. Pulling the reins tight, he held the horse steady while she brushed his coat.

"Do you ride?" he asked, noting how she watched the horse for any reaction.

"No. Only if pony rides at the state fair or a carriage ride through Central Park count."

Stuart wondered what she looked like as a child, and it led him to wonder what they might be blessed with. Both of them were dark-haired and -eyed, both tall and athletic. He felt himself twitch under the denim and pulled his mind back.

"Are you afraid of the horse or just no interest?" Somehow he didn't think she'd be afraid of much. No, instead, he was learning she was careful to study before leaping. The garden was a good example.

"No availability, basically." The horse took a step back, then forward, his tail flinching as he did. Kadence took an automatic step back.

"You're welcome to ride here at the lodge." Her gaze caught his and held for a second too long. He saw the excitement in her look along with a slight apprehension.

"Thanks, maybe someday. I'm still getting used to their size." Again her hand slowly ventured toward the animal, and she softly patted his neck. And again Stuart hardened at the sight, wanting her hand to be on him instead of the horse.

He laughed at himself and let his thought fall from his lips. "Size frightens you?" Holding her look, he waited to see if she'd take his bait.

"Only in certain categories," she tossed back, letting her eyes fall to the junction of the horse's back where his legs were spread. Automatically, he drew one leg up and blocked her vision. His move made her laugh openly at him. Kay waited for him to qualify her answer. When he didn't, she added, "You started this line of questions. Want to stop?" Her dare wasn't lost on him.

"You're a double-edged sword, Ms. Farrell, but I'll give you this one. Seriously, if you want to learn to ride, this is a perfect place. Private trails and the animals are usually well-behaved. The late afternoons or early evenings are my favorite time to ride."

"Somehow I don't think it's as easy as hop up and go."

"Let me know when you decide. I'll have one of the men teach you. A few hours and you'll have the basics. Then you can make an educated decision whether to go further or not." Again he caught her look, and she studied him as if he were issuing a dare.

"No thanks. First I'd like to do some reading on the subject. Then I can make an informed decision. I like to do my homework."

"It's a good idea. At least you'll know what you're getting into." Stuart heard the catch in his own voice and added, "And you won't regret it if it doesn't work out?" Kay took a step back and shielded her eyes with her hand, blocking out the last moments of daylight that guarded his expression. She studied him before speaking, and he watched her eyes flash at him.

"Are we still talking about learning to ride a horse?"

"In a manner of speaking." His grin could only be construed as maniacal. "Let me know what you decide. If you're interested, I'll get somebody to help you."

"I'd rather choose my own teacher, if you don't mind." She cocked her head to one side and let the tip of her tongue run over her bottom lip. Stuart knew Kay knew exactly what she was doing, and he couldn't stop watching her intently.

"That might be dangerous on several levels!"

"Define which ones… It's the only way to make an informed decision."

Stuart drew a breath and looked down at her. While they'd bantered, her hand had relaxed against the horse and was now stroking his ear casually. He couldn't decide if she was just teasing him and messing with his head or if she was doing it on purpose. Either way, he knew she'd won this round and he wasn't willing to continue the conversation in his current aroused condition. Bursting at the seams didn't begin to explain his situation. Staring down at her cleavage wasn't helping. He knew he had to get away from her or he'd drag her up on the horse with him and take her into the woods and show her just how to ride. The chill that ran through him was visible, and she didn't hold back her smile.

"It's getting late. The mosquitoes will be out soon. We can explore those levels another time."

"Maybe. Thanks for the offer. I'll get back to you. Good night, Stuart." She turned and walked slowly up the side staircase, then along the balcony that fronted the four apartment doorways. She knew he was watching and turned to him. "Wood or metal?" she called down to him.

"Wood or metal horses?" he asked, teasing her.

"The cabinets for your house," she told him with an exasperated smile.

"Wood." He only got a nod in return. No good or bad, no smiles or long faces. As usual, she had him tied up in knots.

* * * *

Kay waited long enough to watch him turn his horse in the opposite direction and spur it into movement. In the shower with her eyes closed, her hands became his, and she knew the small release she'd brought herself was nothing compared to what he might do to her. The idea gave her goose bumps as she dried off.

It was early enough to drive the half-hour into Wilmington. Kay decided to get away for a few hours. Maybe take in a movie.

Anything to get her mind off Stuart and how he made her feel, how he made her want for something she wasn't sure existed.

* * * *

Tonight her cart held only a few special plants, all flowers. There were several flowering hanging baskets, and she was deciding where she could put one of them when he moved beside her.

"We've got to stop meeting like this every Thursday," Stuart teased. Freshly showered, the blue work shirt and clean jeans only enhanced his full frame. His hair was still damp at the edges, and she wanted to run her fingers through it.

"I'll start coming on Wednesdays if it will make your life easier," she teased back. Not knowing what to do next, she waited, and so did he. Finally, she started to laugh.

"Good lord, would you look at us. Two intelligent adults who can't seem to find the words to be civil to each other when what we really want…" His eyes flashed at her, and she felt the heat brush across her chest and inflame her neck and cheeks.

"What do you think I want, Kadence?" His voice was low, the words spoken close to her ear. She drew a breath and smelled his soap. "Tell me."

"You already told me, that night in the kitchen," she said defensively. He took a step back when his hand reached toward her cheek, just missing contact with her skin. Her eyes shuttered closed as he moved away, knowing he'd shut down again.

"Have a good evening, Kadence. Drive carefully." He slipped away quietly, leaving her dumbfounded in the garden center once again. She forgot about the baskets and ultimately pushed the cart to the side, gathering up the few plants she'd already chosen and making a beeline for the checkout. Only after she was safely locked away in her car did she calm down. It was ridiculous, really. Talking to herself all the way back to the lodge, she argued both sides of their case, just as she had every legal case she took on. In the end, nothing changed. She was attracted to a man who happened to be her boss and apparently who didn't have strong enough feelings for her to do anything about them. With renewed enthusiasm for her self-imposed celibacy, she resigned herself to getting on with the job instead of the man. The job was what was important. In a year, she'd decide where she wanted to go next, but for now, the experience she was gaining was golden. Travis was giving her more responsibility with each week, and she was enjoying the challenge. After a few nights of reading up on the finer points of horsemanship, she'd let Stuart know when she was ready to ride.

* * * *

He found her sitting in the pen with the dogs. Some nights he watched her with them from a distance, wishing he was the one she stroked instead of the beagle. On those nights, he forced himself to move away quietly. Tonight should have been one of those nights, but after their last meeting in the garden center, he'd felt bad about the way he left things with her. He knew she heard him approach; the gravel walkway under his boots gave her time to realize she wasn't alone. Standing on the outside of the kennel, he spoke quietly.

"Good evening, Kadence."

"Evening, Stuart." They were the first words that had been passed between them in over a week. Kay's hand rose to her chest then fanned her face. He decided she didn't realize her actions, but he noted her nipples budded through the cotton shirt she wore. "Chloe's getting big," she added, sounding lame, as if she were searching for a neutral topic. Hell, he was hoping not to embarrass himself. In the last days he decided he wanted her, then not, seventeen times over.

"She's gonna get bigger," he whispered, trying to sound normal.

"Will it be the first birth at the lodge?"

"Yes." He hadn't thought of it from that perspective. It lightened his mood to think of new life on the land. “Brunch went well today.”

“Thanks, the team makes the difference. We’re all getting to know each other a bit better, all working in a better rhythm now.”

“Any problems I should know about? Anything to help you settle in?”

“No, but thanks. I’m quite comfortable in my apartment and with the job. Anything you’d like to revise?” She watched him catch her words and look away.

“Just checking.” He wanted to tell her yes, he’d changed his mind and he wanted her in his bed. That she’d managed to bury herself in his mind and he’d not been quite sane since they met, but he didn’t and wouldn’t.

Kadence stood and brushed off the back of her jeans. When she reached the fence, Stuart unlocked it for her and watched as she slipped past him. So close, he wanted to touch her. They stared at each other for seconds before she spoke.

“I overheard the guys talking about running the dogs tomorrow.”

“Just practice. I have a new radio system I want to check out.”

“I’ve never seen dogs hunt,” she started and then looked away. Apparently she hadn’t missed how his shoulders stiffened at her insinuation. Letting out a slow breath, he decided it wouldn’t do to embarrass either of them further. It was quite obvious he didn’t offer to have her join him. “Good luck with the test,” she finally said, adding, “See you Tuesday.” She walked away quickly but stopped several yards away from him. “Will Chloe run tomorrow?”

“No.” He took off his hat and slapped it against his thigh, the dust settling in a light cloud around his hip. She didn’t answer, just started walking again. When he knew she was out of his sight, he let himself breathe again. “Damn her,” he said.

Stuart stayed with the dogs for a long time, berating himself. He had ignored her when she asked to come along, pretended he didn’t get her inference. He wanted to kick himself several times over. But he also knew if she was along, the radio wouldn’t be the only thing tested. His willpower would be on the line, and in front of the crew he didn't want to have to deal with his emotions on view. Only now that he'd effectively turned her down, again, he really wanted to kick himself. It seemed he'd been wrong about her and Travis. They were good friends, but they didn't seem to be romantically involved. Yes, they laughed and hugged, but Travis was always away on his downtime. And twice Stuart had run into him in town, both times with a woman, a different woman at that.

Still, he felt she wasn't an option. No woman was for him, even if she was tall and dark with curves and a killer smile. Even if she was the first woman in a long time to make him actually feel again. And then he knew what the problem was. Kadence Farrell made him feel again, and that was dangerous territory. Emotions had always gotten the better of him in the past, and he'd managed to stay unattached and unencumbered these past years. That was how he liked his life, sane and settled. Or at least how he liked it until Kay came to the Lodge. Best to just get on with his game plan, he reinforced to himself.

Only lately it was getting harder and harder to do just that. Even the plans for his home were on hold until he made some final material decisions, and he hadn't made those choices yet. Deep down he knew why he was holding off, but it wasn't rational. Building his home should be his domain, so why was he holding off with the details of the kitchen? The answer kept coming back and slapping him over the head. He was waiting to figure out how to get Kay's input. He wanted her to be comfortable in the space he would finally build. He laughed resignedly at himself. Hell, he couldn't even talk to her most of the time without getting tongue-tied and an erection. He'd ignored each of her attempts to get closer, yet here he was picturing her in his home, their home. The irony wasn't lost on him, just unappreciated.

Chapter Nine

In the weeks that followed, life at Agrarian Lodge became crazed. They were full to capacity and had taken on several part-time staff as well. Kay had seen Stuart in passing mostly. With both guest houses full as well as the lodge, she'd been pressed into longer hours. In summer the guests who went fishing on the lake boats always took lunch, and it was now Kay's department to handle. While it was part of her expressed duties, the first weeks she was there, the waters had still been cold. In the last two weeks, the fishermen had arrived and cold or not, they were going to fish! This left Kay working three extra hours each weekday. Her days flew past, her lazy afternoons a thing of the past.

Stuart was still keeping his distance from her, and she decided to just write him off as a possible sex partner. In the few hours they had off duty, she and Travis had taken a few motorcycle rides, his knowledge of the area making him a great tour guide of back roads and quiet beaches. On one such outing Travis pulled the bike to a secluded section of sandy beach, allowing them privacy and quiet to watch the gentle tides peaking against the shoreline.

"You're not happy lately, Kay. Anything I can fix?"

"Not in the kitchen," she told him, laughing. "I'm just horny, and self-satisfaction just isn't cutting it anymore." Kay knew her answer would create a situation that might turn sexual and let out a sigh. "Okay, we had an agreement to just be friends, but…"

"But you're not getting anything from Stuart, and I'm the next best thing." He said it with a smile, but she wondered if his feelings were hurt.

"I've had strange thoughts lately, Travis." She finally took off her helmet and got off the bike, walking to the shoreline. He moved beside her, and Kay decided to be honest. "I know this isn't what you want to hear, but lately I've had…fantasies about both you and Stuart doing me."

He turned to look at her with a smirk on his lips. "At the same time?"

"Yes. Is that terrible?"

"No, just not something I've done lately. Years ago Stuart and I shared women. It wasn't a big deal, it was just sex."

"And the idea of it now?" She stared directly at him, waiting for his answer.

"Is intriguing, but I don't think Stuart is in the same head space."

"He seems to think we're still having sex, and he doesn't want to invade your territory." Kay hesitated. "I'm guilty of the crime in his mind, so I might as well be getting the advantages, if you're interested."

He burst out laughing and dropped his arm around her shoulder. "As long as you understand I'm not the marrying kind."

"Travis, you've never been the marrying kind. I don't want to get married, I just want to have sex without strings—that's my philosophy since the divorce." She dropped her hand to his crotch and covered his hard-on. "It seems you're of the same mind."

"I'm always ready for sex with you. I've just backed away because I see how Stuart looks at you. I didn't want to get in the way of the two of you."

"Apparently there isn't a two of us, so why should we both deny ourselves?"

"We shouldn't," he pronounced, taking her hand and walking her back to the motorcycle. "Are you game for an adventure?"

"With you, yes, anything you want."

"I want to lick you. It's been too long since I tasted you."

"Talk like that will get you laid, my friend."

"That is the plan." He maneuvered her so she was resting her butt on the seat of the bike and leaned in to kiss her. It all came back, his size and scent, and she became instantly enamored by him as she had the first time they met. It was the way his large hands wrapped around her head and tangled in her hair, tugging her toward him. He wasn't gentle but seemed to know instinctively just how rough to tempt his fate. Kay slid her arms up his shoulders, pausing to test his muscle strength with her fingers. As she pinched his upper arms, his tongue thrust deeper between her lips, and she greedily accepted his probing, pushing her body harder against his.

Travis had always been a heady experience for her. He made her want to be bad, to cross the imaginary lines and let him have his way totally with her. Kay's body betrayed her feelings, her nipples hard and aching. She'd never felt her pussy so wet, so wanting, her lips puffy and full. How could she begin to tell him what she wanted? It had been so long since they'd been together, it was almost like being with a stranger, yet safer. His demeanor allowed her to feel the pure, unadulterated lust she'd tamped back for so long, along with a bit of curiosity thrown in.

His lips left hers and trailed a line of kisses down her jaw and across her neck, each feather kiss sending a shiver down her spine, ending directly in her pussy.

"What are you up for, Kay?"

She had to clear her throat to answer, her voice lost to his touch. "I'm not sure," she finally managed to answer, staring at his face, memorizing each feature. "I've been out of circulation for so long."

Grabbing his hand she moved it to her breast, an act of silent permission. His hand immediately covered her tit, his hand large enough to encompass the entire bulk, squeezing and releasing while she moved against his body, jutting her hips against his hard-on.

"Travis," she whispered, and moved his other hand to her other breast. She dropped hers to his crotch, sliding up and down over his bulge. His jeans were pulled tight, the material straining against his cock. The harder he pumped her breasts, the harder she palmed his dick.

"If we're gonna do this, I want something," he told her, hesitantly taking a step back, her hand falling away. Kay was disappointed that his hands weren't on her breast. He'd just started pinching her nipples, and she wanted him to use more pressure. "Don't move," he told her and moved around the bike, starting the engine to a low roar. Instantly the image of them fucking the first time came to mind, and she was intrigued. "Nobody can see us here, nobody can hear us. Just relax and enjoy, Kay. Let go, nobody will ever have to know."

His words circled in her mind, and she suddenly began to wonder if this was a terrible idea. By the time her thoughts cleared, he'd stripped down her jeans and panties, pausing only to tug off her shoes until he could strip her bottom half naked. There was no time for second thoughts, but she glanced around to reassure herself that they were truly alone. Kay let him lift her onto the seat facing backward, easing her to rest her shoulders between the handlebars. Tugging her by the hips, his fingers bit into her skin as he repositioned her to lie along the seat, spread wide for his taking. Travis stepped to the back of the motorcycle and straddled the rear tire.

"Oh, baby, I forgot how magnificent you truly are. You have a beautiful pussy."

She watched him lick his lips and rub his hands together. With one step, his face was between her thighs. He started light, rubbing his late day five o'clock shadow against her skin until he finally ran a line of kisses down her inner thigh, pausing to change sides, repeating the kisses. "You're wet already, Kay, wanting this."

"Yes," she managed, and realized she was pulling up her shirt and fumbling with her bra to free her tits.

"That's it, baby, pinch your nipples for me and watch the sky." He disappeared between her thighs, and she felt that first probe of his tongue at her pussy. He took long licks at her lips, then short ones before nibbling at her clit. Kay didn't know how long they stayed that way, and she didn't care. She had this amazingly handsome, sexy man licking her pussy and telling her to relax and watch the sky.

Kay felt no shame in palming her own breasts, tweaking her nipples until they were harder than she'd ever felt in front of a man. "Travis, finger me," she told him, realizing her words were verbal and not just in her mind.

"One or two," he teased, watching her from between her thighs.

"Try me and I'll let you know." She heard him laugh, but immediately his tongue was back probing at her pussy. His hands were flexing around her thighs, and she felt one slide down, felt his hand rubbing along her lips. "Travis, don't make me wait." He didn't, pushing his thick index finger in her pussy. Kay came instantly, felt her body clutching his digit, and wanted more. "Another," she asked, and he instantly complied, easily sliding his middle finger beside his index finger inside her. Between his licking her and her climax, her body felt fluid and hot from his touch.

"Kay, you are one hot bitch, literally, to my touch."

"Save the conversation, just lick me till I come again, and then you can fuck me." She knew she'd said the words, was slightly stunned then realized she didn't care. She'd made the decision to enjoy this experience. He continued fingering her pussy and nuzzling her clit. He withdrew his fingers, and she groaned in disappointment. It was only temporary as he repositioned her on the bike. His fingers immediately went back to her pussy. "That's better."

"The lady knows what she likes."

"The lady wants to feel your cock inside her."

"Where?"

"In my mouth to start, but ultimately in my pussy."

Travis moved his hand, and she knew she had asked for it but wasn't happy. He came and stood beside her head, pausing to open his jeans and push them down his thighs. "God, you're huge," she told him, grasping for his erection and guiding it toward her mouth, licking the first droplet of pre-cum. "Long and thick," she said on an outward pull.

"Stay there," he directed her and shifted his position. She could just suck his cock while he fingered her pussy lips, just missing the penetration she wanted. But to have complete control of his cock was exhilarating. To have the pulse of the engine under her did almost all the work. She simply held him between her lips, and the engine idle moved him in her mouth. Kay slid him back and forth between her teeth, never letting him completely fall from her lips. He groaned several times, jutting his hips to go deeper down her throat. She sucked him greedily, loving how she could control his orgasm. Of course, that meant he controlled her pleasure, too. But to see the pleasure on his face was her reward. She shifted to take him deeper and tightened her fingers around his base.

"Fuck me before you come." It took a few seconds for her words to register, and he finally took a step back, fumbling in his pocket until he pulled out a condom. He didn't waste time, simply tore the package and sheathed himself. He reached for her hand and put it on the throttle behind her head. With his fingers pressed to hers he twisted it slightly and the engine roared. "I get it." Travis moved to the back and straddled the tire, pulling her forward to meet him, sliding his cock in her pussy in one smooth motion. It was exquisite how her body stretched to accommodate him, absorbing each thrust.

"Christ, you're tight. I figured I loosened you with my fingers, but…"

"All the better for you," she said, and twisted the throttle, his words lost to the roar. Kay didn't know how long he fucked her. All she knew is that she was mesmerized by how her body reacted to him. She grasped at the handle for balance, and it twisted further, sending pulses of energy through her. Kay came, grasping his cock with her inner muscles, milking him deeper inside her. He groaned and stilled.

"I'm gonna come, Kay."

"Go ahead, you deserve it, earned it."

Travis thrust several times more, and she felt him surge deeper inside her. She was so relaxed, she didn't care she was spread naked over the seat of a motorcycle in a parking lot at the beach. All that mattered was the act and the result. Not to disappoint, he went back and licked her again, using his fingers to punctuate his tongue flicking her clit. Kay came again, but it was barely a shudder, her body exhausted and sated like never before. She dropped her hands from the throttle and reached for him. Travis paused to hitch his pants back up to his waist and with a few steps, dropped his leg over the bike and lowered his body over hers. This kiss was flavored with her cum, and she licked his lips clean. "Thank you."

"You're welcome. How about we get a drink, some food, and then I'll fuck you again, this time in your ass until I'm ready to come. Then I'll pump on your tits and lick them clean."

"Promises, promises," she teased, trying to gracefully get out of the position she was in without unsettling the motorcycle.

"Food first, Kay, then…" He grinned at her and stepped over the bike. Travis reached to the ground and handed her jeans and undies up to her, which had to be turned right side out before she could attempt to put them on. He watched each move as she dressed, smoking a cigarette and chuckling as she tried to pull her bra back over her puffy nipples.

"Let me suck your cock hard and see how fast you get dressed."

"Later, it's time to get out of here." He helped her to right her shirt and held her balance as she put her shoes back on. "Come on, Kay, let's eat, and then I'll eat you."

"What more could a girl ask for." Kay went with him willingly, hopeful for the rest of the night's activities.

They never got back to sex. After dinner at a seafood restaurant on the way back to the lodge, they discussed Stuart.

"You realize we just proved him right," she told Travis while they feasted on boiled shrimp and cold beer. "Don't get me wrong, I enjoyed our afternoon, but I bet tonight he'll be looking at us cross-eyed when we get back, as if he knows what we did."

"I've known him a long time, Kay. He's never been jealous, so that tells me he does have feelings for you. You have to decide how you feel about him."

"Travis, I don't want to get married again. You of all people know what went down with my divorce. Why can't I just have a relationship with him and occasionally ask you to join us in bed?"

"It works for me, but with you, Stuart seems…obsessed."

"I suppose it doesn't matter. Being with you today proved his point and mine. I want the freedom to fuck both of you. I'll take my loss of his touch, but I'll cherish how you made me come this afternoon."

"At your service, ma'am, whenever you need the release."

"As long as we're away from the lodge and Stuart doesn't find out. I just don't want to live with his 'I told you so' look for the rest of my time there."

"I know you'll move on after the contract, and I understand why, but I am enjoying having you in the kitchen with me."

"Me, too, I like my job. It's a shame we couldn't just find a happy medium for all three of us."

"With time, my dear, sometimes things change. Besides, you want Stuart as your mate. And you just want the freedom to invite me to join in occasionally." He stared at me with a strange smile.

"What?"

"Just a curiosity, what if Stuart gives you a counteroffer?"

"Such as?"

"Well, if he decides to let you enjoy him and another man, what would you say to him asking another woman to join you?"

"You're a troublemaker, Travis, and enjoying this too much. And you know the answer. I've had my experiences with women. I enjoy women, but I don't get the same sexual turn-on as I do with men. Besides, some women get jealous, and that's what I'm trying to avoid. If Stuart asks another woman, most likely she'll think she should get all his attention. I'm into cocks, fucking and sucking them. Women, even with toys, just don't have the same just effect for me. Call me indelicate, but if he offered a woman with a cock, I might be interested!"

Travis burst out laughing. "Been there, done that, as you would say. I think if he knew in advance the woman had both sets of equipment, he'd make an informed decision. But I wouldn't spring it on him as a surprise."

"I suppose that's another issue not to mention to Stuart. But can I ask you a question?"

"We've always been blunt, go ahead."

"When you and Stuart used to share women, did you share each other too?"

"No. We've had a third man who serviced us once, but Stuart and I are both into women. We did better when we shared just one woman and gave her our attention."

"So I guess we just aren't meant to be a threesome."

"Not just yet, but you never know with time."

Chapter Ten

Kay knew come October the fishing would dwindle and she'd get her afternoons back after hunting season closed at the first of the year, but the difference left her exhausted in the evenings. Which was a good thing, she decided. It kept her from having too much time to think about Stuart Drake. After her last fiasco of inviting herself to see the dogs practice and having him ignore her, she'd gone to town and gotten a library card. Now, when she had spare time she spent it in the cool room filled with books. The short drive relaxed her, and she especially enjoyed reading the out-of-town newspapers.

The head librarian, Grace, was rapidly becoming a friend. About her age, she'd been born and raised in the Wilmington area, coming home after college with a broken heart. The following year, she'd taken the job and hadn't looked back. While Grace didn't seem to date or at least tell Kay about her dates, they enjoyed lunches together on Mondays when Kay was in town. Occasionally they'd meet for a movie or to shop in the early evenings. Tentative still, Kay understood that friendship developed over time, and she was just happy to have a female friend to talk to occasionally, even if they weren't to the "baring your soul" stage.

Happy with her job and especially with her performance at it, she had fallen into a comfortable routine. Travis lavished her with praise often, and even Stuart had stopped by several times to compliment a certain lunch or dessert. It didn't slide past her that he always made a point of doing it when there was other staff present. He still hadn't mentioned anything about her garden and neither did she.

Travis was using, with regularity, the fresh herbs that she was growing. She had small vines of tomatoes and cucumbers growing up stakes Hoyt had brought her one day to supplement the chicken wire. While he ignored the garden mostly, occasionally he would take her aside and give her a tip or suggestion. She welcomed his input and even earned an occasional smile from him. Only Stuart kept his distance, and she figured it was for the best.

Kay knew Travis and Stuart often had men's night out on Mondays. She never asked where they went or let on that she even knew. Only Martha's occasional comment gave her inside information. She still swam most evenings while the guests were eating and had done some research on riding a horse. Kay hadn't mentioned to anyone that the idea was appealing to her.

The only problem she had to deal with on a daily basis was Jimmy Timms. He was summer help, signed on for May, June, July, and August to run the fishing boats. As captain, he oversaw the other marina staff as well as maintenance on the boats. Her contact with him was limited to lunches for their guests as well as the crew. Kay had smiled and laughed at his attentions in the first few weeks he was working there. It seemed to her he was always in the kitchen, standing just a bit too close for her comfort. Many a time she turned directly into him. While trying to maintain a professional tone, she'd asked him to refrain from being in her space while she was working, telling him she'd run him down one day. He laughed and nodded at each request, yet always seemed to be too close. He hadn't been outright rude toward her, but she knew the warning signs.

By the second week, he was reaching to touch her shoulder or arm, and she found herself pulling back sharply. By the beginning of the third week, she'd had enough.

She was tired and hormonal and hot. It was her last nerve he got on that morning, standing close behind her and running his fingers along her neck. It sent a sick chill through her, and she lost her composure. Kay swung around so fast his coffee sloshed over the rim of his mug.

"Don't touch me, Mr. Timms, ever again. Do I make myself clear? I've asked you repeatedly to stay out of my workspace, and you insist on dogging my every step. Now you've made me spill coffee on you. Please keep a proper distance!" She'd held his look and waited for an answer. His eyes had squinted while he stared at her, deciding how to answer. Kay kept her stance, not backing down. Unfortunately everyone else in the kitchen had overheard, the noiseless space invading their standoff.

"Sorry, baby," he started, and she took a step closer, narrowing her eyes toward him.

"I am not your baby or anything else to you. From now on, unless you have business that pertains to the guests' meals, I'd prefer it if you kept your distance from me. Both at work and off." Kay knew she should reign back her tone and didn't. She'd had enough of the playboy and his leering ways and his innuendos that made her feel dirty after he'd left. He was always just short of being crude with her.

Lisa intervened, ending the staring standoff between them. "Mr. Timms, is there a problem with the meals?"

Both Kay and Jimmy had turned to look at her, Kay thankful for her presence.

"Just getting some morning coffee," he replied, with a slimy grin.

"Then you have no reason to be pestering Kay when she has so much work to do."

"Now, who says I was pestering her? We were just teasing each other," he started, only Kay jumped in before he could continue.

"No, Mr. Timms, I'm not joking or teasing with you. I'd prefer you kept your distance physically from me, do you understand? Your only business with me is about lunches, and that's supposed to be handled by e-mail the night before. If there are any last-minute changes that need to be handled, please call from the dock. I'll not stand for you in my workspace any longer." Her tone had become courtroom low, her eyes daring him to look away. For a pregnant pause, all three of them stood quiet.

"Hey, I don't need the hassle. It's your loss, babe," he tossed over his shoulder as he left the kitchen. Kay relaxed her posture and smiled at Lisa.

"Thanks, I can't stand him always breathing on me."

"You should have told me sooner," Lisa said.

"I figured a few rude comments and he'd back off. I was wrong, obviously."

"Men. You just can't figure them out." Lisa turned away and left quickly. Kay was glad for her backup this morning, but when she saw Travis later in the day, she made a point of telling him about the episode in case there were any repercussions. He promised her he'd keep an eye open and not to worry about Jimmy.

* * * *

Kay sat on the ground in the second kennel, stroking Chloe's ears. She'd been moved a few days earlier because they weren't sure of her due date, only that it should be close. Stuart had said he wanted her sequestered from the rest of the dogs but not isolated. She'd heard his footsteps on the gravel walkway before she saw him.

"Evening Stuart," she said, letting him know she knew he was there.

"Kadence, how's she doing tonight?" He didn't enter Chloe's pen, only commanded the rest of the dogs to be quiet while they spoke. Finally, he let himself in and petted the dogs, keeping the fencing between him and Kay.

"She seems stressed, or maybe just tired. I suppose if I was carrying a litter, I'd be tired too."

"Did you want a family?" he asked out of the blue, surprising her with his question.

She didn't hesitate to answer, and she seemed to stun him when she did.

"Yes, I do. But when I realized my choice of husband wasn't

great, I made sure it wasn't an issue." She watched Stuart and wondered what he was thinking. Had his thoughts gone back to the telephone conversation he'd eavesdropped on and understood her rationale? She added, "At least I wouldn't have been carrying five or six."

Stuart laughed. More like seven or eight." Kay gave him a horrified look and broke into laugher as she stroked Chloe's belly.

She knew Stuart watched her hand and wondered if he was debating how she'd stroke him. He left the dogs quickly, giving her a brief good night as he did. Kay laughed at his quick retreat.

* * * *

Kay sat with the dog a little longer, wondering what had sent Stuart running this time. Shaking her head, she said, "He's just afraid of me," talking to the dog who only stared at her. "Maybe you have the right idea, old girl. Just do the deed and move on." Kay stood and dusted off the back of her jeans, only to turn and realize Stuart was still there.

"I'm not afraid of you, Kadence." His voice was a low growl.

"Could have fooled me, Stuart." She left the pen and locked the gate, forcing herself to confront him.

"You should be…" he started when she got closer to him. Kay was sick and tired of playing this game with him. First Jimmy this morning and now Stuart.

"Men!" she said aloud as she pushed past him, only to have his arm come out and stop her progress. He looked at her, and she held his gaze, not flinching or backing down.

"I'm not afraid of you, Stuart, on any level. I'm an adult who makes my own choices. You've made it quite clear that I'm not yours. So let's just drop the pretense and move on." Again she refused to look away, instead staring down at his large hand on her upper arm. Kay figured he was deciding what to do or say and was disappointed when he dropped his hand from her. Her arm immediately felt cold where his fingers had held her.

"Why didn't you tell me Timms was bothering you?"

"Because I wanted to handle him on my own." She watched him before adding, "Did Lisa tell you?"

"No, Travis mentioned he was annoying you. I'll speak to him tomorrow."

"No, don't. It will only make it worse. If he starts up again, I'll let you know. Hopefully with Lisa's intervention this morning, he'll back off." She hesitated, then laughed. "I lost my temper this morning. I don't think he'll want anything to do with the shrew that confronted him today."

"You have a bad temper?" he asked, laughing at the concept.

"Just don't piss me off," she told him. "Seriously, he's like a child; the more you warn him away, the more he'll pester me. Just drop it for now, and if he starts up again, I'll handle him differently next time."

"And how will that work?" he asked, seriously wanting to know.

"If he touches me again, I'll drop him." She said it with clarity and intent. She stopped to wonder if Stuart accepted she could do it.

"I'd love to be a fly on the wall for that," he said, laughing openly.

She watched him intently and shook her head. "You have a wonderful smile, Stuart. It's a shame you don't use it more often. Or is it only me that you stiffen around?"

"Stiffen is an appropriate choice of word, Kay." His look dared her to top him. Stuart watched her carefully.

Waiting to see where she took his statement, Kay decided his expression was one of silent agony. "At least we know I can," she told him. With a half laugh, she started to move past him. "I'm too old for games, Stuart. I've turned into a selfish woman. I want what I want when I want it without complications."

"I'm too old, too," he whispered and surprised her by pulling her against his body and dropping his mouth over hers, his lips warm against hers. He tasted her rather than plundered into her mouth as she'd braced for. Anger she could deal with. Tenderness she wasn't ready for.

His kiss continued, with the tip of his tongue sampling her lips until he finally let the tip of it skim between hers, meeting her tongue in a tempting dance of passion. Kay opened to him and let her hands glide up his chest, resting on his shoulders as he pulled her closer to him. His excitement was evident against her, hot and bulging. She felt a warmth flow through her she hadn't felt in a long time. It was different from how she'd felt with Travis, but it was still the same sexual tension building inside her that had a small groan escape from her throat.

Her hands reached to fist in the back of his hair, pulling him closer to her, flattening her breasts against his chest. Stuart pulled back to look at her and, with a mumbled curse, went back a second time. Prepared for him, Kay took the kiss she wanted, the kiss she'd been thinking about when she was alone with her thoughts. His groan told her she was doing something right, and she felt him shift her over his erection, his hands moving her hips to stroke them both.

Kay decided Stuart had lost his mind and didn't care. He would feel the heat from her body slip to him as he used her to stroke against himself. In a moment of tense clarity, he pulled back from her a second time, his head dropping on top of hers, holding her against him still, but gasping for air and control.

"Damn it, Kay," he whispered, his hands moving her head to look at him. "Now do you understand why I keep my distance? I have no control around you," he said, just before his lips took hers in another round of erotic foreplay. When he pulled back this time, his hands thrust her from his body. She almost stumbled from his actions, his hands steadying her before he let go. "Kay…"

"Let it go, Stuart," she said, forcing herself to move a step farther away. "I'll try to stay out of your way from now on," was barely a whisper, and she quickly moved away, uncomfortable with the arousal he flamed within her. From a safe distance, she turned and watched him for a moment, his fingers crushing the wire fencing beneath them.

* * * *

Kay knocked loudly on Stuart's door, her hand automatically twisting the knob as she did. While her knock was loud, she tried to keep her voice down. "Stuart, wake up, Stuart…" The knob moved in her hand, and she didn't hesitate to push the door open.

In the dark she saw his shadow in the bedroom doorway, his sheets twisted and one pillow lying on the floor. She didn't stop her eyes from taking a long, appraising look at his bare chest, following the line of swirling black hairs that led her gaze lower, noting that he'd pulled on his jeans and zipped them but hadn't buttoned them yet. For three seconds, Kay forgot what was so important she'd barged into his apartment.

"Kay, what's wrong?" Stuart froze as she looked at him, letting her have her look. His hand ran through the top of his hair, pulling it from his eyes. "Kay?" He was awake. She had to pull back a small smile after realizing she was staring at his nude chest.

He took a step toward her. Stuart's expression was blank. He didn't know what to think. Was something wrong, or was her visit meant to go in another direction? He watched as she visibly shook herself from the blank stare and flashed to his face. Thankful there was no light on, she'd have waged even odds that she'd blushed when she realized she was checking him out.

"It's Chloe," she told him and backed from his private space, leaving without another word.

* * * *

Pulling on his boots and grabbing a work shirt from the drawer, he was downstairs quickly, but he knew she'd run back to the barn. Even with an almost full moon, he couldn't see her in the distance. Stuart let himself have his self-serving smile as he cursed himself for thinking she'd come to him for…him. By the time he reached the barn he knew she was there, her voice in the distance soothing Chloe.

"It's going to be okay, girl," he heard and knew she'd be petting the animal. His animal started to stand at attention, and he shifted his cock in his jeans before walking to the last stall he'd moved the pregnant dog to a couple of day ago. He'd wanted her to be warm and safe and away from the rest of the dogs when she gave birth. And it seemed she was in the throes of doing just that. Leaning on the stall door, he took in the sight.

Kadence sat in the far corner on the bed of straw beside Chloe. Her hand gently stroked the dog's head, her soft words continuing. "That's a girl, just breathe, Chloe."

Stuart shook his head and moved closer to them. With Chloe on her side, panting heavily, he saw she was ready to deliver. He knew there was nothing he could or should really do for her at the moment. He'd let nature take its course and hope for the best. Kneeling before her, he too started to talk to the dog.

"Okay, Chloe, you played, now you're gonna pay, girl." Kay shot him a look that a lesser man would have shied away from. "What?" he asked. "Technically, I'm correct."

"You make it sound like she had a choice to use birth control and didn't."

Stuart shook his head, laughing at her. She started to tense, and Chloe turned her head, feeling the difference in her attentions. "Sorry, girl," she crooned. "Men. What do they know?" She continued staring at the dog. "If this one knew what was good for him…" Kay paused then he turned away.

* * * *

Stuart walked away and turned on a few of the overhead lights. For the next two hours he and Kadence sat beside the dog as she delivered and cleaned her pups. Not until all seven were nestled against a nipple did Kay finally rise from her spot, stretching to her full height, her hands going to her aching back, after praising Chloe.

"You're a good coach," Stuart told Kay.

"Thanks, but Chloe did all the work. I just cheered her on a little." She smiled at Stuart, her eyes heavy. "She was probably wishing we'd leave her alone."

Stuart reached up and pulled several strands of hay from her shoulder. "What do you wish, Kay?" He was close, too close, and he was too tired and too emotionally wound up to deal with her. He knew if he touched her now, she'd most likely melt into his arms and push him for the completion they'd ignited within each other.

"Stuart, this isn't the time for word games. I'm tired and overemotional after watching the births—just let me go."

His finger traced the line of her chin, and she angled against his touch, her eyes closing. Stuart took her by the upper arms and gently pushed her back against the barn wall, his eyes intent on her. His lips barely grazed hers, and he suddenly pulled back.

"Go to bed, Kay."

Her eyes flew open, and she saw a strange look on his face. "Stuart?"

"Kadence, leave now, or I won't be held responsible." His voice quaked when he said "responsible." Slowly, she slid to the side and away from him, but she hesitated.

"I wanted to check on the dogs one last time." She looked as if she'd just come from his bed, and he wanted it to be true.

Stuart's words were almost growled at her. "Kay, go to bed, damn it."

She stiffened at his tone, all but running as she turned and left.

* * * *

After a shower, she dropped onto the bed thinking about the hours they'd sat with the dog while she gave birth. It was a lesson in restraint for her. Too many times did she want to reach toward him, to touch him, and didn't. Stuart had stretched out on his side, an arm's length from the dog and her. He, too, soothed the dog, his large hand checking her belly occasionally. The action had hit her on a core level she hadn't known she possessed. In that very instant, Kay wanted to know what it would feel like to have his child growing inside her, to feel his hand protectively warm them both. Sleep didn't come, only frustration she wasn't able to conquer. By four, she was up and dressed and had dough rising, the smell of coffee wafting through the whole kitchen.

* * * *

Stuart had showered and dressed and gone to his office. He didn't attempt to do any work. Instead, he dropped on his couch after forcing Harley to relinquish it, and couldn't believe he'd sent her away, again. Only knowing she'd been right when she said they were tired and emotional had he managed to find the restraint to hold himself back. What he wanted to do was drop her on a fresh pile of hay and show her what he wished for, prove to her that he could satisfy her and hopefully prove to himself that he could still live without her afterward. Only that small degree of doubt allowed him to keep a clear head. Once he and Kay were together, Stuart knew letting her go wouldn't be easy. Beyond the fact that she was his employee, he didn't want her to go away.

The situation annoyed him. He wanted her close, but knew he couldn't touch her. He wanted to touch her, but knew once he did she'd never leave his mind again. It was difficult enough in these last months to stay sane with her around. Stuart knew himself enough to know she'd be imprinted on his soul once they were intimate together.

He let out a cynical laugh, realizing he was now thinking *when* instead of *if.* Closing his eyes, he pictured her lying beside the dog, her thin T-shirt not covering her braless state.

She'd mentioned that she woke from a strange dream and went to check on the dog. That was when she'd gone to get him. While she'd pulled on jeans, he noticed she didn't wear any socks, her sneakers were untied, and her hair was loose around her shoulders, only finger combed. Her rumpled, sleep-heavy eyes dared him to reach out and stroke her breast, dared him to make her nipple come alive under his touch.

Stuart had found himself wetting his lips, and he'd forced himself off the stall floor. He'd rummaged around to give himself time to subside and came back with several old horse blankets to cushion where Kay lay. She accepted them gratefully and dropped beside the dog quickly.

* * * *

The smell of coffee brewing drew him to the kitchen. He knew it would be Kay. Taking a deep breath, he moved quietly into the space, only to find it empty. Filling a mug from the half-empty pot, he walked to the back door and looked out. On the top step sat Kay, cradling a mug between her hands. She was dressed for work in jeans and a white cook's jacket. Her hair was braided down her back. Only the occasional movement of her shoulder let him realize she was crying. As soon as he opened the door toward him, she spun around. When their eyes met, she looked away, using the back of her hand to wipe her cheeks. Stuart moved behind her after pulling several sheets of paper towel from a roll nearby.

"Here," he whispered and dropped the toweling into her lap. He stood against the doorframe while she blotted and dried.

"Thanks." She didn't turn around to look at him.

"Are you okay?"

"Yes, just tired and on puppy overload, the whole miracle thing. Relax, Stuart, I'm not pining for my own children just yet." Finally she turned and winked at him. "I still have a few conquests to explore."

"Oh, now I'm a conquest?"

"In a manner of speaking. But don't get all shorted up about it. I know my preferences might not be the same as yours."

Stuart felt his cheeks heat with embarrassment as his cock stirred under his jeans, pulling the material tight, his bulge obvious. Clearing his throat, he changed the subject. "I'm going to walk over to check on her—want to come?"

"Yes, please." Kay stood and managed to blink back her tears. He didn't mention them, and she didn't, either. They both left their mugs on the top step and drifted slowly toward the barn. Inside, it was quiet and dark. Only an occasional tail swish or snort could be heard. As they neared Chole's stall, Stuart didn't open the door, rather leaned over. Kay did the same.

"They look like hamsters or gerbils," she told him.

"I agree, but give them a few days."

"Are you going to keep them?"

"I'm not sure yet."

"I know she's not human, but it seems a crime to take her pups from her."

"It won't be for weeks yet," he said.

"I know. It's not a rational way to think about them. They're…dogs."

"Somehow that you see her as more doesn't surprise me."

"You knew I liked animals."

"Yeah…" Chloe looked up at them but didn't disturb her family. Instead, she seemed content to lie there and nurse them. "Could you imagine nursing all seven?" he teased.

"I have enough trouble picturing me nursing one at a time."

"I don't. I can clearly see you with a baby to your breast."

Kadence obviously didn't know what to say, so she defaulted and said nothing. When the silence stretched between them, she pushed back from the stall door. "I have dough rising. I should get back."

"Kay," he started, and she turned to give him her full attention. Dark eyes stared at dark eyes before he spoke. "If I kissed you earlier, I don't think I would have been able to stop there."

His admission rang true, and she managed a small smile. Instead of debating his not kissing her, she changed the subject for which he was sincerely thankful. "Thanks for sitting with us."

"I'm glad you came and got me."

"Me, too." With that, she turned and left him in the barn, watching her take long, purposeful strides away from him.

Chapter Eleven

Kay stood outside Stuart's office door, her right hand wrapped in a dish towel filled with chipped ice. She'd managed to stop crying and was just pissed now. Automatically her right hand lifted to knock on the door, but she hesitated, switching to use her left hand. She heard a muffled "In," and threw open the door.

Stuart was behind his desk, the telephone to his ear when she first saw him. He stood slowly in reaction to her appearance and hung up the phone. Kay didn't heard him say anything, he simply dropped the receiver onto the cradle and moved slowly around the desk toward her.

"Kay, what's happened? Are you all right?" He moved cautiously near her and then behind her and closed the door.

She knew he watched her whole body heave with each breath she took as he glanced at her from head to toe. She knew she must look a mess but didn't care. Her hair was pulled from its braid, the shoulder of her T-shirt ripped at the seam. Her jeans were dusty and her face was dirty and tear-streaked. She'd paused to clean up as she passed through the kitchen but decided not to wipe away any evidence.

"Kay, come sit and tell me what happened. Do you want a doctor?" he asked cautiously.

"*No,* I want…I want…I want to break something."

He watched her glance around the room but didn't move, and neither did she.

"Kadence, take a breath and tell me what happened."

"Jimmy Timms happened. He cornered me in the barn."

Stuart's eyes glanced back to her face as his hands gently reached to her shoulders, and he waited to get her look.

"Kay, I'll take you to the emergency room," he started, and she laughed at him.

"Don't take me, but you better take him!" she said.

"What's going on? From the start, Kay, don't leave anything out." He moved her to the sofa and all but threw Harley onto the floor. She started to holler at him for treating the dog that way and stopped mid-sentence, letting her body drop to the worn leather. Stuart sat beside her but left space between them.

"I was visiting with Chloe and the pups. I heard a noise and wasn't happy when I found Timms leaning on the stall door." She swallowed hard and pushed back another round of tears. Frustrated, she stood and started pacing the length of the office. "We had a few choice words for each other. I've come to learn Mr. Timms doesn't take rejection well." She managed a half laugh but didn't continue.

Stuart went to the cabinet on the far wall of his office and pulled a bottle of scotch from it, splashing some into a crystal glass. He moved back to her and held it toward her. At first, she shook her head and didn't reach to take it.

"He wouldn't let me out of the stall… I knew better than to let him come inside."

This time when he held the scotch out to her, she took it and downed it in one shot, handing him back the glass. Stuart didn't hold back the surprised look on his face but didn't verbalize his thoughts. Instead, he poured another shot in the glass and again handed it to her.

"Slowly, this time," he whispered. "Kay, tell me what happened. Did he hurt you?"

"No, I wouldn't let him. He told me the price to leave the barn was a kiss." She let out a string of muffled curse words and didn't care that Stuart heard them. "Needless to say he didn't get his kiss."

"Where is he?" Stuart asked, moving from beside her. It was then Kay noticed his hands balled into fists.

"Stuart, I didn't come to you to protect my honor. I came to you because I might have hurt him. He could probably press charges against me if he chose to."

"Just what the hell happened out there?" His hand ran through his black hair, the strands separating around his fingers. Even in the tense moment, Kay visualized Timms on the ground and half held back a laugh.

"I told you, he wouldn't let me out of the stall, and I wanted to leave. I more or less explained to him in physical terms that he wasn't going to stop me."

"Kay, exactly."

"He grabbed at me, and I threw him." She looked at Stuart and smiled. "His mistake was getting up." Suddenly she started to laugh. A few tears slipped out, but by now she didn't care that he witnessed them. As she calmed down and the scotch filtered through her system, she let her guard down. "God, Stuart, you should have seen his face when he hit the floor. I warned him not to get up."

"And?" He took the glass from her hand and drank half of it before handing it back to her. "And?"

"And he didn't listen. I was almost out of the barn when he grabbed me from behind." A revolted chill ran through her, but she went on. "It was the second drop that got him."

"How, Kay? And please be specific."

"For the police report?"

"No, for my visual pleasure," he teased, apparently hoping to joke her into relaxing. It worked, and she sat back, moving the ice on her knuckles back into place.

"I flipped him over my shoulder and to the ground a second time. He grabbed my leg and pulled me down over him. My knee connected with a tender part of his anatomy!"

Stuart didn't hold back the cringe that went through his body as he almost felt the hit. "Let me see your hand."

"It's all right, just bruised."

"From hitting him in the…"

"No, his jaw."

He stood back and gave her a questioning look.

She jerked her left shoulder. "Jaw first with my fist, crotch second as I was trying to get up."

Stuart looked her dead-on, and she could tell he knew she'd given him the second shot on purpose. His smile told her without words he'd have done the same.

"Remind me not to piss you off. I don't want to be on the receiving end of your wrath." He attempted to laugh, but it fell short. "At least you were clear enough to fight off your attacker." He carefully took her hand and unwrapped it from the towel. Her knuckles were red, the skin broken on three of them.

"I'll be fine," she started, pulling her hand from his grasp. She allowed him to rewrap it before kneeling down in front of her.

"Kay, did he…"

"No, Stuart, I told you, I wouldn't let him touch me. The only reason I'm here now is because he really might press charges against me. Beyond being dropped by a woman, I dented his ego…literally!"

"No, he won't." Standing, Stuart lifted the telephone. He made one call in a whispered tone.

"Stay here," he started, but she stood up beside him.

"Oh, no, it's my confrontation, I'm going with you. If he wants to make a big deal about it, I'll be glad to file the necessary attempted assault charges against him."

"Stay here, Kay, please?" His patience was wearing thin, and she knew it.

"Stuart, if I send you in to confront him, I'll never know any peace here. I have to do this myself. I just wanted…backup and witnesses."

The office door was flung open, and Hoyt and Travis moved into the private space. Both of them took one look at Kay and started asking questions. She managed to calm all three men and reinforced that she wanted to confront Timms and have it out, but she wouldn't mind them standing beside her, as long as they let her do the talking. Kay was quite persuasive in making them understand it was important to her that she take the initiative and retain control.

They found Timms on board the speed boat, a bottle of beer in his hand. His jaw was red, but other than that, he didn't seem injured. He watched the four of them approach the boat through slanted eyes and started cursing at them all.

"Shut up, Timms," Stuart started.

"What, she had to get her boyfriend and the rest of the gang to come and beat me up?" He said it with a shrill laugh, and Stuart stiffened beside her. Kay gave Stuart a warning look before pushing in front of him.

"No, they're here as witnesses. Are you planning on pressing charges?" They all watched as the idea flickered around his mind and a sick smile crossed his lips.

"It's a possibility," he told them.

"Fine, then let's all go to the sheriff's office right now."

"Now, hold on, little lady," he said, stalling when he realized she would go.

"Don't call me anything other than Ms. Farrell, Mr. Timms. This isn't open for debate. Do you want to press charges against me or not? Yes or no? Because if you do, I want to give my statement and get the charges against you on the record. Now."

"You want to tell us all what happened, Timms, your perspective?" Stuart said.

They all watched as he decided how to handle them.

"It was just a misunderstanding between Katie and me."

At the same time, Stuart told him not to call her Katie, and Kay said, "Don't call me that," causing both of them to look at each other. Neither watched Travis or Hoyt taking in the whole scene.

"Mr. Timms, are you injured, and are you planning on pressing charges?"

"I think…"

"Yes, you should think very carefully." Stuart took a tall stance and braced his weight. "If you want to see the sheriff, we'll go now and you can explain why you cornered my chef in the barn and wouldn't let her past. And you can explain to all the deputies how she dropped you, twice." Stuart's voice left nothing to chance. "What's it going to be?"

"Let's just leave it as an error in communication."

Timms wasn't happy, Kay realized, and knew her trouble with him wasn't over. But she knew enough to take one situation at a time.

"Fine, as long as we understand each other. Don't ever attempt to touch me again, Mr. Timms. I won't be held responsible if you try again." Even Travis took a step back from her tone. She hoped the look on her face betrayed how dangerous she could be.

"Kay, do you want to press charges or drop it?"

"As long as he stays away from me, I'll drop it. But I expect a wide berth from you," she warned before turning and walking away. The men didn't follow her, and she refused to look back.

She walked back to her apartment, showered, and started to feel better, cleansed from his touch and breath. There was a light knock on her door an hour later, and she tensed, wondering who it would be. Travis stood on the other side, a bottle of amber liquid in his hand.

"I figured you could use this about now. I know I can," he said as she let him into her apartment.

"I'm fine, really. I just wanted him to understand I wouldn't let him get away with it." She didn't hold back the lilt in her lips peeking into a smirk.

"I didn't know you had martial arts training," he teased.

"I don't," she told him with a smile. "Instinct, pure instinct," she said and let herself have a good laugh. "And a little New York street smarts. I rode the subways."

From the doorway Stuart's voice entered their space. "Is this a private party, or can anyone come in?"

"Come in, Stuart," she said, rising to get a third glass. "Join the party."

He entered her apartment for the first time since her arrival. She saw him glance around, seeing how she'd decorated the space. From her perspective, her books and computer gave it character. The throw pillows and afghans she'd tossed around gave it depth. Kadence handed the extra glass to Travis to fill and went back to her seat in the old rocking chair under the window. While they all talked around the evening's excitement, she finally brought them back to the subject.

"You three didn't hurt him, did you?"

"No," both men answered, but she could tell they had wanted to. It endeared them both to her just a bit more.

"I've given him a formal warning. He's not to go near the kitchen for any reason, and he's to leave any place you happen to be if he gets there." Travis avoided her look.

"Travis?"

"We never touched him, rather explained what would happen if he ever went near you or any of the female employees again."

"It's not just you, Kay." Stuart looked uncomfortable. "This is technically my fault. He cornered one of the waitstaff last week. The girl told Lisa about it, and I had a talk with him then. If he does anything like this again, I have full rights to fire him."

"That would screw up the summer. You know it, and he knows it. Where are you going to get a replacement with no notice?"

"I'm hoping not to, but it's the least of my worries if he keeps harassing my staff."

Travis cleared his throat but didn't add anything to the conversation after Stuart shot him a look. "This shouldn't have happened, I'm sorry."

"So am I, to a point," she said, adding, "Did the waitress…"

"No, she started crying, and he panicked." Travis started to laugh, and so did Kay.

"If I'd known that, it would have saved my knuckles," she said.

They all knew she was trying to defuse the situation and the anger in the room. Stuart was taking the incident to heart. They managed to get through their drinks, and she yawned blatantly in front of them. Travis took her hint and rose, stopping to drop a light kiss on her forehead.

"See you tomorrow, Kay," he told her as he left, not looking back to see Stuart hadn't moved from his seat.

"Night, Travis, thanks for the backup tonight."

He gave her a mock salute, hesitated, and finally left.

"I'll go, too, Kay. I'm really sorry this had to happen."

"It's not your fault Timms is a jackass. Besides, now that he knows I can take care of myself, I doubt he'll look in my direction again. I'm bad for his ego." She started to laugh and silently cursed herself for letting her eyes fill. "I'm fine, Stuart, just the aftershock," she told him, but she didn't push him away when he walked to her and pulled her up out of the chair and into his arms.

"If he hurt you, I'd have killed him," he whispered into her hair.

"Don't let him know he bothered me. It would only fuel his warped mind."

"Screw him and his warped mind, it's you I'm upset about. You shouldn't have to fight off another employee on my land."

"Well, let's hope it's the last time." She started to pull back, and he didn't let her. Instead, he held her as if his life depended upon it. Kay realized she liked being held by him and forced herself to take a step back.

"Will you be able to sleep?"

"I think so," she said, afraid to look at him.

"Kay, we're going to have to discuss…"

Her apartment door was flung open once again, and a now drunk Mr. Timms stood watching their embrace.

"Not good enough for the hired help, set your eyes on the boss man instead," he slurred at them.

Stuart automatically pushed her behind him when he turned around. "Timms, this is off-limits to you. We just had this discussion on the pier."

"Yeah, well," he said, his hand making a strange pattern in the air, "I figured I'd come and apologize to the lady, didn't expect to interrupt her with you."

"Get out and stay away from here." Travis was behind the man, his words hissed into his ear. Timms turned and realized he was outnumbered, putting his arms in front of his face to ward off any impending blows.

"Travis, get him out of here, please," Stuart asked him, adding, "I'll be along in a minute."

It was easy for Travis to take Timms by the arm and half drag, half pull him from Kay's doorstep.

"Lock this behind me, Kay. Nobody will bother you tonight, I promise."

She started to speak, but Stuart didn't wait. Instead, he moved to the balcony and whistled for Harley. The old hound ambled toward him and he reached down to pet the dog. "Guard Kay," he said, and the dog lay at her doorstep. She held back a smile but reached down to pet Harley.

"Thanks, Stuart. I'll be fine, really."

"I'll see you tomorrow, Kay."

"Good night," she whispered, and his fingers came up to trace her cheek.

"Don't unlock this for anyone tonight. Is your cell phone charged?"

"Yes, I'll be fine."

"Then get some sleep," he told her and moved away from the door.

Chapter Twelve

The next morning Stuart stopped by the kitchen just before the rest of the breakfast crew was due to arrive. He made no pretense of getting coffee. Instead, he moved directly to Kay and reached for her right hand. While her knuckles were bruised, her hand was only slightly swollen. They both stared down at their hands without saying a word. Stuart pulled her to his body with his free hand and held her against him.

"I don't know what I would have done if he hurt you." His voice was strangled as he tried to say the words.

"I won't let him hurt me."

"I won't, either, I promise you, Kay." His lips grazed her cheek, and he pulled back abruptly. He dropped her hand and backed away, leaving the kitchen. Harley stayed at his spot on the back steps.

* * * *

Kay had managed a few hours of sleep but was grateful that the old dog was waiting for her when she woke. He ambled alongside her on the dark walk to the lodge kitchen, a walk she never had a second thought about. This morning it seemed every shadow had her on edge. While refusing to allow Timms to intimidate her, she realized he would be a problem. And she knew she'd be prepared for him if he chose stupidity over common sense.

Kay figured she'd see Stuart at some point during the day but never expected the level of emotion he showed her. It left her with an odd feeling all day. Later that night, she automatically went to visit

Chloe and hesitated. Harley was beside her still, having become her shadow all day. Instead of skipping her visit, she threaded her way back to the lodge and to Stuart's office. His door was ajar and the room was empty. Now she had to make a decision. Did she go to the barn alone or back to her apartment? She realized if she let him, Timms would intimidate her to no end. She would not let him drive her to be apartment bound. Chloe won out, but Kay felt better with old Harley beside her. Entering the darkened space, the smells of the barn filled her nostrils and brought back glimpses of conversation she and Stuart had shared while sitting with Chloe as she birthed her pups just days before.

Kay thought of how relaxed Stuart was, stretched out in the stall just out of her reach. While he was able to reach to the dog, she was just beyond, a metaphor she didn't miss. They had laughed openly about her aversion to blood, and Stuart told her life is messy in general. Questioning him further, he used Chloe as an example.

"Not pretty to look at, but think of the new life that's struggling to survive."

"Easy for you to say—you'll never have to give birth."

"No, you're right there, but think about it from a male perspective, Kay. We plant our seed and relinquish all responsibility to the mother. Even if we wanted to participate, the process is taken from our hands. All we can do is sit by and watch, hoping it all turns out right in the end. If that's not nerve-racking I'm not sure what else is."

"You're a control freak, Stuart Drake," she told him, tossing a handful of straw in his direction.

"Got it on the first try, Kay." He watched her with an intensity she hadn't seen before and wondered where his mind had drifted. Speaking in a hushed tone as Chloe pushed another pup from her womb, Stuart looked at Kay. "I can tell you I'm not good father material. I didn't have one to emulate."

"Are you angry with the service or life in general that he died when you were so young?"

"Both, and my mother to some degree for not being stronger."

"Maybe with you taking over she didn't have to try to be." If she'd hit him with a boulder, he wouldn't have been more surprised. Somehow Kay figured she'd crossed an imaginary line and pulled back. Stuart dropped the subject, and they fell into a compatible silence while the dog continued her birthing.

"Why did you come here, Kay. All joking aside, why?"

She dropped onto her back for a few minutes, thinking how to answer him. She decided the truth was for the best. It was just the degree of truth she vacillated over. Rolling back, she propped her head on her hand and watched him.

"I sometimes wondered if I'd like to run a bed-and-breakfast. Coming here would give me some time in a reasonably close setting to decide if it was right for me. Beyond having a bake shop one day, I figured I might be able to incorporate both, if the location was right. Either way, it was experience in my field of choice, good, bad, or indifferent.

"Why the lodge for you, Stuart? What little I know about you, I'd have figured you'd want something with little or no human complications." This time it was Stuart who hedged. "Well, don't I get an answer?"

"I wanted to live someplace that wasn't urban for a change. And even though I had the capital, a spread like this needs lots of cash to keep it up. I wanted to be able to have the horses and the dogs. I always liked to fish and hunt."

"So taking in boarders on a weekly basis just keeps the overhead covered?"

"Something like that, yes." He hesitated, and it gave Kay time to study him. "Kay, I'm not the nine-to-five kind of guy. Baseball worked for me until I blew out my shoulder. Even the computer stuff I got into worked for me. There was little pressure to perform on someone else's time schedule. I wanted a place where I could live on my own terms. The lodge seemed like the best of all worlds put together."

"So living on your own terms is your point of contention. But the responsibility factor, you've never been able to walk away from that, have you?"

"No, not altogether, but for me this is the best of all worlds. And to paraphrase you, 'If you're not the lead dog, the view never changes.'" He laughed, and it went straight to her heart. "I'm not cynical about it, I just like to be in charge. I like things done my way and…"

"And heaven forbid anyone has a stray thought?" She managed to hold a straight face for all of three seconds before bursting out laughing.

"As you so eloquently put it, I'm alpha male material. Can't teach an old dog new tricks, as they say, so on my land, what I say goes. Anyone who has a problem with that is free to move on. My days of jockeying for position are long gone."

"I'm afraid mine are just starting." They watched in silence as Chloe licked at one of her pups, and finally Kay finished her thought. "I went back to school because I knew even if I went with another law firm, I'd never be in charge. If I wanted to open my own office, well…"

"Well?"

"Let's just say the thought of it wasn't appealing enough to make me do it. I'm like you in a certain way, Stuart. My body lives naturally on a different time frame than most. I'm up early and awake. By noon I'm starting to lag. I love a half-hour nap in the afternoon." Kay laughed aloud. "Could you see me telling a judge I couldn't make afternoon court because it interfered with my sleep, or my assistant telling a client that I don't take meetings between two and three?" Again she laughed. "I always found baking relaxing, no matter what I was making. Kneading dough can be very therapeutic."

"So what happens next?"

"I'm not sure. I'm still not convinced running a B & B isn't for me, but the location would have to be right. Maybe just a bakery, it's too soon to tell. In the meantime, I get lots of hands-on experience and training here."

They fell quiet, and she wondered if she'd gone too far. But better he know her true personality from the start, as an employee or as a prospective love interest. Of course, she was jumping in all directions. He'd have a say in that, too, and from what she was learning about him, he was still jealous of her relationship with Travis, even though it had been casual. Kay decided any relationship beyond employee with Stuart would be intense. She remembered how gentle his hands had felt on her shoulders last night in the office. How intense he'd become when he thought she was hurt. She could only imagine how he might be as a lover. She got an instant twinge of heat in her pussy, and her nipples hardened at the idea he might one day suck them. If she was very lucky, one day she might feel his cock inside her.

She shook herself from the memory as she walked closer toward the stall where the puppies currently resided.

A noise at the far end of the barn got her attention as well as Harley's, and the dog let out a low, warning growl. Stuart moved into view with a large stainless steel water bowl in his hand and laughed aloud at his dog.

"Harley, you old fool, don't you recognize me? It's only been one day." The dog sat beside Kay, his tail thumping on the floor. "Come, boy," he said, and the dog bolted toward him. Thankfully the bowl was empty, or the water intended for it would have been showered down on both of them when paws hit Stuart's shoulders. "All right, down, boy, down." Harley gave his face one more sloppy lick before dropping to the floor. Slowly, Stuart moved away and took up his place next to Kay.

"How's your hand?"

"Fine," she started, and then laughed. "Sore as hell, but well worth it."

She moved toward Chole's stall and leaned on the door. Seeing that mother and puppies were all snuggled together, she let out a sigh. Stuart came to stand next to her, his arm dropping over her shoulders.

"I wasn't sure you'd visit her tonight," he started.

"I stopped at the office first, but when you weren't there I decided I wouldn't let Timms chase me away."

"Good, just don't get too lax for the next few weeks. I'm working on getting a replacement for him,"

"Stuart, don't fire him because of me. I can handle myself."

He turned away from her, obviously uncomfortable. "Actually, I found out this afternoon that he's been crowding some of the other women. Apparently the waitress was just another in his quest."

"What a sleazy…"

"Yeah, well, keep your fingers crossed. Hopefully he won't be an issue for long."

They stayed watching Chloe and her family for a long time without speaking. Finally Stuart spoke, but it wasn't what Kay thought she'd ever hear. "If you're free on Monday, would you spend the day with me, Kay?"

"Doing what?" she asked, her bluntness not lost on him, his small laugh told her.

"I have to make a final decision on the kitchen. I hoped you'd look over my shoulder and make sure I don't make any glaring mistakes."

"Why not let Travis check for you?" Still she hadn't turned to look at him.

"Because I'd rather spend my day off looking at you than him," he told her, just before his arm pulled her to him and he let his lips drop down onto hers. Kay accepted his kiss and pushed for one that she wanted, turning their moment into a deeper experience than Stuart seemed prepared for. Pulling back from her, he smiled.

"You don't make it easy for me, Kay."

"Is that what you really want? A malleable female with no opinions or depth?"

"God, no. But maybe you could just cut me some slack occasionally."

"That you have to earn," she said with a devious smile.

"Kay, tell me no, and I'll leave you alone."

"I don't want you to leave me alone. God help me, Stuart, I…" Kay couldn't believe what she'd almost said aloud, thankful she was able to control the impulse to tell him she wanted him inside her.

"You…?"

"I'd love to help you with the kitchen plans."

He laughed aloud at her diversionary tactic and was careful when he took her hand. "Got time for a ride? You should see the site so you can visualize it all better."

"Okay," she said, not surprised when Harley followed them out to Stuart's pickup truck. The drive was relatively short, but she liked how he'd left forest land in between the lodge and his home site, sequestering it into a private enclave. When he pulled in at the end of the dirt road, they automatically got out and wandered the cleared lot. He gave her a brief description of what he was going to have built, and Kay asked questions galore before he moved to the truck, coming back with a pad and pen, jotting down their thoughts as they talked through potential problems with style and design. Finally, overloaded with questions, he threw up his hands in defeat.

"I give up, Kay, no more for tonight."

"All right, I'll go lightly on you, but Monday…" She didn't finish her thought when he moved behind her and pulled her back to his chest. He kept his hands wrapped around her waist and leaned close to her ear.

"Thanks for your help tonight," he said, his breath teasing her ear.

"You're welcome," she answered, locking her hands over his. "Stuart?"

"I don't have a clue, Kay. If you want me to back off, I will, but…"

"No." They stayed that way for a long time that night, Stuart leaning on the hood of his pickup with Kay bracketed in his arms in front of him. The river lay beyond, and Harley slept in the back of the pickup. Kay wondered how long they might have stayed that way if they hadn't been interrupted by his cell phone. Begrudgingly, he answered it, and she knew something was wrong. With a few terse words, he told the caller to phone the sheriff and he'd be right there.

"Get in," he told her as they scrambled into the truck.

"What's wrong?"

"Timms!" He glanced at her only briefly then turned the truck around and sped down the dirt road toward the marina.

"Stuart?"

"I'm not sure, something about a guest and Timms. Lisa was short with details." They arrived several minutes later to find an upset middle-aged woman sitting in the passenger seat of Lisa's car at the dock. Her wet hair was plastered to her face and neck, her clothes still damp. She had a blanket thrown over her shoulders and was staring out at nothing, not acknowledging the people around her. Timms was down at the end of the pier with Hoyt and Travis. It was eerily quiet when they got out.

"Timms offered her a sunset cruise while her husband played cards with the other guests." Lisa paused, nodded her head to the side, and only continued when they all took a few steps from the female guest. "It was supposed to be an hour's cruise, and she apparently thought there were going to be other people with them. Timms had made a move, and in a gallant attempt to get away from his advances, she jumped overboard and swam back. Thankfully the woman realized her error in judgment near the dock."

Just as they were getting this information, a sheriff's deputy pulled up. Kay watched from the side as he and Stuart shook hands and spoke in hushed tones for several minutes. Finally, Stuart asked Lisa and Kay to take Mrs. Ott back to the lodge to clean up, saying they'd be there shortly.

Kay brewed coffee while Lisa helped the woman to her room. She returned dry and composed, with her obviously angry husband at her side. The deputy asked her if she wanted medical attention, and she'd said no. She wasn't hurt, just pissed at Timms. Kay and Lisa both knew how she felt. It was while they were setting up a tray to take to the study that Lisa told Kay Timms had cornered her once, too. She'd been able to get away by telling him she'd fire him, but not before he'd grabbed at her, too. Kay's sense of well-being on the land was shrinking fast. While she wanted to question Lisa further, circumstances didn't allow it. Kay realized just Lisa admitting it was a big step.

"The man's a menace and should be sent away from anywhere there are decent women." Mrs. Ott's voice filled the space and they all looked at each other. While Kay didn't offer any explanation of her encounter, it was an odd moment for them all.

Ultimately, hours later, Mr. and Mrs. Ott decided not to press charges. However, Stuart still fired Timms on the spot. With backup from the deputy, they'd explained clearly to him that he was never to set foot on Agrarian Lodge land again, under any circumstance. They waited while he packed his gear and then saw him off the property. The deputy came back inside to assure everyone he'd make sure Jimmy Timms's reputation was known around the area. It was the only way to keep someone else from hiring him and having the same problem. He also told them if Timms did step back on Stuart's land, he could press charges that would send him to jail for a spell, adding it might be the catalyst to keeping him away permanently.

Later that night, Stuart, Travis, Lisa, and Kay sat in Stuart's private office, sharing a brandy when the fuss had died down. Timms was gone and hopefully never to be heard from again. Mrs. Ott seemed unaffected by the incident, rather viewing it as a story to take back home. How she'd been singled out by a younger man and how she'd swum from his boat to save her honor. Mr. Ott was remaining very quiet about the whole thing, and Stuart made a note to call his lawyer in the morning just in case that changed.

For the first time since she'd been working at Agrarian Lodge, Kay watched Travis sit next to Lisa and drop his arm around her shoulder. With a halting breath, he questioned her.

"Why didn't you tell me this before? I'd have..."

"Yes, you probably would have. You'd have found him and beaten him up. Well, Travis, I don't need you to protect me. I handled him and the situation."

"I know, but still..." Travis stopped when he realized the tone and level of his voice.

Lisa watched him intently before bursting out laughing. "Why, Travis Polson, you old dog," she said and leaned over to kiss his cheek. "You really do care, don't you?" His face and neck turned a bright pink and he didn't have to verbally answer. "Come on, walk me home and we'll talk about it," she teased.

For Kay, it was the first time she'd seen the woman really smile. It was a pretty smile, filled with sweetness and a hint of the devil. Kay hadn't appreciated her before, but the new Lisa emerging before her had spunk. They left not holding hands but giving each other meaningful glances. Once they were gone, Kay dropped onto the couch and started to laugh.

"Stuart, what would happen if I asked you to see me home?" She laughed harder at the look he gave her but stopped short when he simply walked past her and shut, then locked his office door. Moving back into the room, he asked her if she wanted another brandy. Her head indicated no, but she got a wave of heat through her as if she'd drank it. He dropped beside her but didn't touch her. Instead, he laid his head back and closed his eyes.

"Kay?"

"Yes, Stuart?"

"I don't have anything remotely honorable on my mind right now. I think you'd better leave." His fingers rubbed his temples, and he sat forward.

"Poor Stu, you've had a hard couple of days, haven't you?" she teased.

"I'm serious, Kay, unless you're prepared to be taken on this couch, you'd better go. I don't know how much plainer I can say it."

She studied him and realized he was on a thin rope. "All right, Stuart, but only because when we finally make love, I'd prefer it to be in a soft, warm bed, not your office floor."

He glanced up at her, and his eyes flashed. "Or over the desk?"

"Next time the desk." Kay reached down and let her fingers trail along his cheek, her fingers stroking his chin. "Stuart, I like your beard," she said, adding, "Someday I want to feel it against me." Her gaze met his for just a moment longer before she straightened up. "Good night, Stuart, I'll see you Monday for our shopping excursion."

* * * *

He sat there for a long time, knowing it was right to send her away and hating himself for doing just that. But with all the problems with Timms, he didn't want anything clouding their minds when he finally got her naked and in his arms. Soon, he told himself, soon, he'd be with her, and then whatever happened would just happen. He'd had ideas, and every time they were together in any sense, his cock overrode his common sense, and all he wanted to do was fuck her until he couldn't come anymore. Kay was turning into a personal problem for him. He wanted to be objective because she was an employee, but in his mind, they were well beyond that. He envisioned them together, as a couple, always in the heat of some sexual moment.

Stuart decided he was going mad, crazed with lust from the first time he saw her. At first she'd seemed forbidden fruit because of Travis, but now he couldn't use that as an excuse. What he had to do was clear his mind and decide what he was willing to offer her beyond sex. Never before had he ever wanted a woman permanently. Worse yet, he knew she was only there temporarily, for an internship as she put it, until she decided what she wanted to do with the rest of her life. Maybe he'd change her mind and she'd stay on.

Just the contemplation of the concept made him break out in a sweat. No, he reinforced to himself, he wasn't the marrying kind, not the forever after man she would most likely want. He wondered if they could just have an affair? But what would become of him when it ended? Would she leave the Lodge, and would it ever be the same place he'd built, would he ever be the same? The thoughts made his mind ache further, and he forced himself to walk outside for fresh air. Just looking up at the stars made him feel better, as if the world weren't closing in on him quite as drastically as he was thinking it felt.

If he and Kay got together, they'd have to deal with the emotions at that time. Spending his time wondering was a waste, for he knew he had no real idea of her personality. But, he decided, it would be interesting to learn.

Chapter Thirteen

Monday turned into a whirlwind of a day, spent in home centers and furniture stores. For Stuart, Kay decided, it seemed an object lesson on shopping. For her it was a small window into the man she was falling in love with—no, she decided, she was in lust with him.

They'd left early in the morning and stopped for breakfast on the road. Kay studied the plans he'd brought along and asked questions Stuart apparently hadn't begun to think about and most importantly, didn't have answers to. She joked easily with him and at times thought they'd known each other for a lifetime. It was easy to accept him dropping his arm around her shoulders as they stood before a display, Kay pointing out the differences in maintenance between Formica and stone counters. They discussed lever handles instead of knobs, and gas cooking as opposed to electric. By noon, they were both overloaded with information and needed to get out of the stores.

Since it was his day, she let him set the tone and the pace. Within her reach at all times was a pad and pen, and she knew her notes would be invaluable to him at a later date. He pulled into a fast-food chicken restaurant and drove her to the local park to have lunch. The soft afternoon breeze made them both lazy after their meal, and it was easy to relax back against his chest when Stuart pulled her to him, his back resting against a large tree.

Kay nestled against him and closed her eyes, wondering what it would feel like to have him touch her. His fingers stroked her upper arms, and he sent a chill through her that radiated to him. He tensed behind her, and she let out a laugh.

"What are we going to do, Stuart?"

"I don't know, Kay. I've never been in this position before." She started to pull away to look at him, but he held her in place. "I've spent my whole life making sure I didn't get emotionally involved with any woman, and now..."

"Now, what? I came along and screwed up your plans?" Laughing lightly, she added, "Reality's a bitch sometimes, Stuart. How are you going to handle it?"

"You're having way too much fun at my expense, Kay." His arms tightened her to him, and she closed her eyes. "The problem is I don't really know anything about you, yet I'm drawn to you, Kay. I don't know why, but I am, and it bothers me to no end."

"Poor Stuart, would you rather I disappeared from your property, and then you could go back to brooding at the world all alone?" While her voice was light and teasing, it held an undercurrent of seriousness.

"No. It wouldn't matter where you were location-wise, you're embedded within me, Kadence."

"If I left, you'd forget me, with time." This time she pulled from his warmth and turned to look at him. "I have no right to make you uncomfortable in your own space, Stuart. Technically, I'm an employee. I could leave and make your life easier."

Studying her face for a long time, he finally shook his head. "It's not that easy. No matter where you were, you'd still be in my mind. Kay, beyond that..."

"We'd be good in bed together, Stuart. But an affair with you would be complicated, beyond our boss-employee status."

"What are you looking for? Why shut yourself away down here when you could work in any restaurant in any town? Why, Kay? That's the piece of the puzzle I'm missing. Help me to understand."

"Because I've done the city thing, and New York was Eric's territory." She let a shudder run through her, and Stuart tried to pull her back toward him.

"What did he do to you, Kay?"

She knew he knew the basics from listening in on her

conversation weeks earlier, but figured he wanted to hear her version, in her words. "It doesn't matter," she started, but he cut her off.

"Yes, it does. Your marriage to him would reflect on ours."

Kay didn't know who was more surprised, her or Stuart, when the words left his lips. She stared at him for a long time and watched his eyes close against her attention.

"Stuart?"

"Let it go, Kay, please?"

She watched him for a long moment before she lay beside him, her head resting on her hand. Her free hand traced along his bare forearm, and with each stroke she became bolder, her fingers learning his skin.

"He cheated on me," she said in a low voice. "He thought I would be moldable into the perfect wife. Educated so I wouldn't embarrass him in front of his business associates, not too hard to look at from a certain perspective. I fit his criteria. What I didn't fit was his attitude toward infidelity. I was supposed to be so happy and grateful that I was the one he actually married, his afternoon diversions weren't supposed to bother me. I was supposed to keep my mouth shut and accept it as a 'dick' thing." She laughed aloud and rolled onto her back. "Obviously, I didn't accept it or keep my mouth shut."

"The man was a fool, Kay."

"Thank you, Stuart. I agree, and I won't get married again unless I feel it's for the long haul and we both understand each other's core values a lot better. But that doesn't mean I'm not looking for companionship and a sexual outlet." She let a few seconds pass before going on and moved back on her side to see him better. "I'm not averse to relationships, just as long as we both work from the same set of rules. Even if they aren't conventional, as long as we all agree to the terms." She watched him stiffen at her words.

"What did you mean by 'we all agree to the terms'?"

Kay gave him a noncommittal smile and rolled on her back, sheltering her eyes from the sun with her arm. At first she'd thought to tease him about a threesome with Travis, but the idea struck her hard, made her pussy wet and made her start to think in different directions. All her life she'd been told marriage and one partner were the accepted norm. Maybe she was different. Maybe she could break the rules as long as her partners agreed. The concept was so foreign to her she almost laughed aloud but accepted this wasn't a joking matter.

Deep in her being, she understood the unconventional might be her best goal. Having Stuart as her lover and partner would be good, and adding Travis on occasion would definitely be interesting, from her perspective. Kay lay there a long time beside Stuart and wondered how he'd react if she told him what she was thinking. Maybe one day they'd be close enough for her to speak her mind. While she and Travis had teased about another man joining them in bed when they first met, they used dildos for a second cock to please her. The idea of two real men's throbbing cocks in her gave her an inner ache like never before. She sighed and wondered what Stuart would think if she brought her toys to bed with them.

Stuart moved beside her and cleared his throat, bringing her back to the moment.

"Was it a difficult divorce?" He'd moved back against the tree to put some distance between them. Kay wondered if he did it on purpose to keep from reaching to touch her. For right now, that was okay with her. She needed to think clearly and with a level head before she let this whole arrangement blow up in her face.

"No, not really. We had a prenuptial agreement." She rolled onto her stomach and laughed, shaking her head. "We were both attorneys. We couldn't have married without one."

"But? I get the feeling I'm going hate this man for something beyond treating you poorly. What did he do, Kay?" It was a long time before she finally spoke, and she closed her eyes momentarily against the memories before she did.

"He got his mistress pregnant." When she drew a deep breath, he held his hands still. She focused on them instead of watching his expression. Somehow she wanted him to touch her but knew it wasn't the time. She didn't want his touch while talking about her ex.

"When I first found out about her existence, I insisted we go to counseling. Only after the first sessions, I was the only one going. Somehow he always had an emergency. That in itself made me wonder about our future, but when I found out Diana was pregnant... He told me he stopped seeing her, and he'd told her I was a shrew wife who he was separated from, but I wouldn't divorce him."

"How did it finally all come to an end, Kay? What was the final catalyst?"

"Diana came to see him one Saturday when she knew he'd be busy. She was going to surprise him when he got home. But, she showed up at the door and was shocked to find me in Eric's apartment. I was stunned at first, realizing she'd been in my home, and I lost it. Just the concept of him taking her there was enough to...but after a few minutes we both calmed down, and over a pot of tea, we cleared the air between us. We both realized he was playing us against each other. It pissed us both off to say the least. When we were able to talk rationally, we pieced the truth together. He'd only brought her to the apartment once, in the beginning of their relationship, two years earlier. God, we'd only been married a short time and he already had a mistress. After that, they always used her apartment. He told her I had his apartment under surveillance to use against him in court. She never questioned him beyond that. Apparently when she did, he'd get...nasty with her." Stuart pushed himself forward at her words, and she shook her head. He let his shoulders fall back against the tree but didn't relax. "He wouldn't hurt me. I was his wife for public consumption. The perfect little woman who kept a home, had a career, and kept her man happy. What a joke it all turned into."

"What finally happened?"

"I asked her for a week, and she didn't tell him about our meeting." Kay rolled onto her back and stared at the sky. "By the following Friday, his clothing and personal items were packed, our bank accounts had been divided, all nice and legal according to our agreement, and the divorce papers were drawn up. I managed to get him alone while he was still at his office late in the day and had my lawyer meet me there." She laughed aloud and turned back to him. "He wasn't happy to say the least. I did everything according to our papers, and he had no recourse. I'd had a fidelity clause inserted, and he was egotistical enough to think I wouldn't use it. When I told him about my meeting with Diana, he hit the roof." Kay studied Stuart for a moment before adding, "Would you like to know how he justified his lying and cheating?" Stuart didn't attempt to voice his opinion, only shook his head. "He told me it shouldn't matter to me, that he was, and I quote, 'just banging her,' while me, he made love to." She laughed openly and rolled away. "Like that was supposed to appease me!"

"Why did you marry him?"

"I was in love and a little bit in lust, too. He was tall and blond with blue eyes and a bad-boy air. The complete opposite of any boy or man I'd ever dated. I was immature enough to think that because he chose me, he'd stay faithful to me."

"You were married. You had a right to believe that."

"In a perfect world, yes. We don't live in anything near perfect, Stuart. I spent several years going through life with rose-colored glasses on because it was easier than admitting I'd made a mistake."

"I don't see you that way, Kay. I can picture you busting your ass to make him a comfortable home, to be the perfect wife. But I also get the impression that you could have been a goddess and it still wouldn't have been enough for him."

"To a certain degree you're right. Eric felt he had a right to cheat, that it was every man's not-too-guilty pleasure. He had the balls to tell me it was a throwback to the old days when men still ruled the home and a wife wouldn't dare to confront the master of their house." Stuart laughed openly at that. Kay did, too. "Obviously, I didn't agree."

"So did he stay with his mistress?"

"Of course. Eric's not the kind of man to be without a woman under any circumstances. He'd view it as being weak."

"Did it bother you that he went with her?"

"No, not really. After I met her, the thing is, was... If we'd met under different circumstances, we'd probably have been friends. She's a very nice woman, just not very smart when it came to choosing a man. I'm guilty of the same thing. I couldn't condemn her for it." He watched her decide and finally continue, her words carefully chosen. "When he called here that night, he expected me to go running back to him. That one call from him years later and I'd drop my life and..."

"I'm really glad you didn't."

"Me, too. Stuart, he told me he doesn't think their baby is his. I don't know Diana very well, but I can't believe she'd have cheated on him. I think he tired of the dad thing and is trying to escape from her and their daughter. The thing is I feel bad for Diana and Dee Dee. Not that Eric is stunning father material, but that she'll probably never..."

"Jeez, Kay, who is this guy, a slug? Do you actually think he'd throw her aside, and especially their child?"

"To paraphrase his words, when the paternity test comes back he'll either have his life back or pay for the rest of it. Either way, he'll want nothing to do with either of them. I don't think Diana deserves this kind of treatment."

"Did he marry her?"

"No, he wouldn't. That's probably what pushed their situation. He probably found another girlfriend and felt tied to Diana. Any excuse to cut and run."

"So you came to the lodge to heal?" he questioned.

"No, I didn't see it that way. I forced myself to stay in New York and go to school there. I could have gone just about anywhere, but I didn't want to let him run me away from home. I liked living in Manhattan. It was a world unto itself. My friends were there, too. I healed myself as much as I was going to during that time. School was a good diversion, and staying in the city was the right choice for me at the time. But when it was time to look for work, I wanted something different."

"Different how?" He didn't expect her to burst out laughing. Kay sat up and straightened her shirt and went about clearing up their picnic and standing. "Kay, is the subject closed?" he asked, rising as she tugged the blanket from under him.

"You'll think I'm crazy..."

Stuart caught her arm and took a step closer to her. "Probably, but tell me anyway." He held her look, daring her to look away.

"Something along the lines of, if you're not the lead dog, the view never changes."

Stuart dropped her arm and said nothing, rather mulling over her words while they walked back to his truck. At the door, she waited while he unlocked it and watched him as he studied her. His head dropped to her lips and his covered hers lightly and just for a short second. Reaching past her, he opened the door and waited until she was seated. Turning to pull on her seat belt, he leaned in closer, crowding her small space in the cab.

"Not crazy, Kadence. I can relate completely. You want to be in charge, but you're not here, Travis is. So why?"

"Experience...and some lead time."

Stuart pulled back sharply from her and closed the door.

Chapter Fourteen

Seated beside her with the air-conditioning pumping at full force, Stuart turned to Kay and asked if she could survive one more stop. She told him with a smile she'd manage, and they were quiet on the drive to the next stop. Furniture wasn't what Kay had thought to be helping Stuart pick out, but she realized he was looking for built-ins and relaxed. His slip about their marriage had stayed wedged in the back of her mind, and she wondered what alterative motive was behind the trip.

She gave her opinions of style and fabrics freely, letting him in on glimpses of her personality as well as learning some of his. He'd taken her to several antique stores, where they wandered and wasted time. Over supper they talked about his home, the drawings beside them on the table. At one point, the waitress was standing beside their table, laughing at them as they debated hotly about keeping the grout on ceramic tile clean. The woman sided with Kay about using it in a kitchen setting and joked she probably just lost her tip. Kay assured her she'd not be penalized for telling the truth, while Stuart looked wounded by the women's conspiring.

"I had a good time today, Stuart, but you've listened to me talk all day and said very little other than what pertained to the house or the lodge. Tell me so I'll understand you?"

On the dark back road, it was easy to let the words come. "Basically, I've already told you. I've been responsible since my father died when I was seven. When I was ten it all seemed overwhelming. I kept the budget, wrote out the checks for my mother to sign, gave her an allowance to live on. By the time I was twelve I'd decided I didn't want to have to be that responsible again ever in my life. I enjoy women, Kay, but I've never considered making a commitment to a single one."

"Yet you've chosen a business that's very hands-on, every detail overseen by you. Isn't that a major commitment?"

"Absolutely, something to lose myself in. But people are too fragile, Kay."

"Did your mother ever realize the position she put you in, forcing you into the alpha male at such a young age?"

He only scowled at her in the dark. They were nearing the lodge entrance when Kay broke the standoff.

"I wanted to open my own bakery, Stuart. But the initial outlays are enormous. Coming to the lodge gave me the quasi setting without the capital outlays. Travis trusts me to run my area of his kitchen. It was the best solution I could come up with beyond opening my own shop. The hours aren't bad, I don't have to take the risks of starting a new business, and the surroundings aren't too bad either. All in all, this job seemed like a perfect answer. And I was ready to leave the city. By staying there as long as I did, I felt I proved to myself and Eric that I wouldn't fold under his pressure. The time was right for me to make a new start with my new career. Any other questions you'd like answered before our truce ends?"

"Is that what we had here today, a truce?" he joked.

"I suppose, of sorts."

"What happens when you tire of our small bakery project? Where will you go then, Kay?" She didn't answer, and he pushed the subject. "Don't you still want your own shop in some trendy little town where they charge five dollars for a cup of coffee and…"

"Stop it, Stuart!" For the first time since he met her, Kay had gotten angry and at him. Yes, the night Timms had cornered her she'd been mad, but not at Stuart. Tonight, her hostility was directed at him.

"What? Did I get too close to the truth? You're using us, the lodge, Travis and me, for a little holdover until you decide what to do with the rest of your life?"

"No."

Stuart pulled into the private driveway of the Agrarian Lodge and killed the engine. He slipped off his seat belt and turned to her. "I need to know, Kay, it's important."

"I don't know anymore. When I first came here I thought it might be a place I could..." She didn't finish. Instead, she released her own seat belt and pushed open the door, the overhead light momentarily blinding them both. She stepped down and started walking toward the lodge, Stuart still sitting behind the wheel. Kay knew when he was following her. She'd heard his door open and close. She didn't flinch when his hand caught her shoulder from behind. She stilled in her steps as he moved behind her, stepping close enough to swallow her against his large chest.

"Why?"

She took a few shuddering breaths and spoke in a low whisper. "Travis," she started, and he stiffened behind her. Kay brought her hands to cover his and tightened them around his fingers. "Travis sent me a picture of you and him the day the lodge sign was hung. Ever since then I wondered what you'd be like."

Stuart couldn't believe what he was hearing. "He sent you a picture?"

"Yes. A copy of the same one you have hanging in your office."

"You took the job because of the photo?"

"I took the job because of you."

Neither said a word and it was a long time before he turned her toward him, his fingers moving her chin to force her to look at him.

"I don't know what to say."

"Don't say anything. I shouldn't have said anything. I took the job for the experience, let's just leave it at that."

* * * *

Kay pulled from him and walked quickly down the road. Stuart started to follow her and didn't. He walked back to his truck and waited for his erection to subside while his mind accepted the concept that she'd come to Lodge because of him. When he finally did start the truck he drove to the barn, checked on Chloe and the horses, and then went to the main lodge. He checked his messages and mail and forced himself from his office. By the time he'd gone back to his apartment, he knew Kay was safely locked away inside hers. Now all he had to do was decide what to do with the information she'd given him.

On one hand, it was a dramatic ego boost to think she'd seen a picture of him and was attracted enough to move to be near him. On the flip side, it scared the hell out of him. Visions of her stalking him floated past him, and he laughed at the concept. But it was still unsettling to him. Accepting that Kay wanted a relationship with him scared the hell out of him. Stuart knew he'd keep his distance from her now. To start anything physical or emotional would only hurt them both when she left. Knowing he wouldn't give her the commitment she was looking for, he knew ultimately she'd leave him and his lodge. What started out as one of his better days was rapidly ending poorly.

The old saying of "Don't ask the question if you don't want to hear the answer" passed over him. He'd asked, and she'd answered. Now it would end any friendship they might have built. Stuart was extremely saddened by his revelation and knew Kay was astute enough to know by telling him her truth, she'd lost him.

* * * *

Kay decided she'd been honest with him, and his honesty about no commitments had been blunt. At first she'd crawled into her lonely bed and cursed herself. But as the night wore on, she started thinking in a different direction.

It wasn't the first time she'd thought this way, but now she was actually seriously considering it. Lying on her back, she had a large dildo in her pussy and was pushing it in and out in small increments as she considered her future. With her other hand, she pinched her nipples, sending currents of heat flashing through her body.

What would it be like, she wondered, having two men in her bed? Having two men in her body? Would they let her take the lead, or would they become demonstrative? Would she like them to be aggressive? Kay reached to her bed stand drawer and pulled out a smaller dildo. She lay back and sucked it between her lips. *I know Travis's cock is larger than this*, she mused, shifting until she slid the second phallus in her anus. Kay twisted her hips until both toys were settled where she wanted to feel them. With a light tug, she moved the toy in her pussy just a bit and felt the sensations shoot through her body. Over and over she'd twist the toy or shift it inward and out until the climax hit her. She accepted it willingly, greedily, twisting her nipple harder to make it last longer. Sated from her respite, she made a decision. One that would set her future at Lodge, for good or bad.

The next night, she made a point of stopping by Stuart's office after supper. With a light tap to his door, she pushed it inward and waited until she got a wave to come in. She waited by the window until he hung up the phone and drew a breath. Better to get this over with than have it hanging over their heads.

"Do you have five minutes," she started, dropping into the chair across from him.

"Of course, what's on your mind?" He shifted a few papers on his desk, but she waited until he settled before speaking.

"I enjoyed our day yesterday, I truly did. I especially liked that we were honest with each other. That being said, I think there's one thing I may have misled you on."

"Go on."

Kay knew she had his full attention. "You mentioned no commitments, and I want you to understand…I'm not looking for commitments in my immediate future. You were more right when you questioned my relationship with Travis. Yes, we'd been lovers, but it wasn't serious. Never will be with Travis. I don't think it's in his nature. But you see, I've learned I don't want any long-term commitments, either." She shifted in her seat but pushed ahead, knowing she had to say the words or forever be damned of her own making. "I'm not explaining this well, but I have a different arrangement for you to consider. I like you, Stuart, in all ways and yes, obviously sexually is the first. But I also want some freedoms of my own."

"I'm not sure I'm following you. You need to be more specific."

"What I'm offering is an open affair of sorts. I'd like to be with you, but with a twist. You see, I've always wanted to experience two men." Kay waited for Stuart to explode, but he sat motionless, seemingly stunned. "I enjoy men and their attributes. But I also enjoy using dildos and vibrators." She stood and walked to the sofa, sitting on the edge to pet Harley. "Since I've been divorced, I've learned a lot about my body and what I want and like. I like the feel of two cocks in me at the same time." She waited until he looked at her. "What I'm dancing around is that if you're interested, I am, without commitments. But you should be aware I will bring toys to bed with us, and my ultimate goal would be to bring a second man on occasion."

"What?" Kay held back a smile at the squeak in his voice. "I thought your husband's actions disgusted you?"

"They did, but that was because we were married, with vows and an understanding of fidelity. When that all blew apart, I decided, since I wasn't married, it would be my call on who I slept with and when. Lately, I've had ideas of how it would feel to have your cock in my pussy and Travis's in my mouth. Or you down my throat and his up my butt."

She stood and walked back to his desk, resting her hands on the shiny surface, bringing her face level to his. "I'm trying to be honest with you. I want to make love with you, and on occasion, I'd like to invite Travis to join us. Not all the time, just occasionally." Kay paused and decided to finish her truth. "Yesterday I told you Travis sent me a photo of the two of you. What I didn't tell you was the instant I saw both of you together, with your arms around each other's shoulders, I wanted to be in the middle of you. Does that make any sense? I wanted to be loved by both of you at the same time."

She reached across the desk and let her fingers run down his cheek, through his beard, and holding tight, she tugged him across the desk. He allowed her to pull him halfway and accepted her kiss. It was Kay in charge, Kay taking him with her on a sensory journey that could lead to endless possibilities. When she released him, he let his weight drop back into the desk chair behind him.

"Well," was all he managed.

Kay walked around the desk and dropped to her knees by his side. She ran her hand along his crotch, pausing to encase his erection with her fingers. Kay looked directly at him and held his gaze. Faster and slower, harder and softer, her fingers moved all over and around him.

"What should I do, Stuart, stop or finish you off?" Kay let go of her grip and watched him gulp for air. The look on his face was total confusion. It was easy to spin his desk chair until he was facing her. Deftly her fingers undid his belt, and she gently unzipped his pants, snaking her hand inside his boxers until she clasped his cock. "Your skin is so warm, so hard," she sighed, leaning forward to engulf him with her lips.

Kay knew this probably wasn't a good idea, but she'd started it and she'd finish the act, even if it was just for herself. She settled her weight on her heels and began to make love to his cock, swallowing him deeper on each pass. His groan told her she was doing something right, as did the droplets of pre-cum she lapped up. As Stuart relaxed back in his seat, she leaned forward, being more aggressive, using her teeth to drag against his skin on each outward pull. He groaned, and she repeated the act, using her hands on his hips to hold him in place.

When she had his cock buried down her throat and her nose pressed against his crotch, she dropped her hand and started to fondle his balls. Stuart shifted his hips farther toward the edge of the seat.

"You like that," she whispered, going back to swallow his cock. Kay suddenly pulled away from him and leaned back. His eyes flew open and watched her. She wiped her lips with the back of her hand and gave him her most provocative smile. Rather than going back to his cock, she paused and slowly unbuttoned her shirt, tugging it off her shoulders and letting it fall backward. Her fingers unsnapped the front clasp of her bra, and it sprang open, revealing her breasts to Stuart's vision and her touch.

She gave no thought to touching herself in front of him, rather made an elaborate process of palming and squeezing her breasts. Pushing them together, she pinched her nipples harder, making her raspberry peaks full and puffy. Keeping one hand on her breast, she leaned forward and captured Stuart's cock back between her lips. She began her onslaught again, slowly swallowing his length while fondling his balls with her free hand.

"Pinch your nipple harder," Stuart told her as he reached forward to touch her.

She pulled back and smiled at him. "I didn't invite you to touch me, yet." Teasing him came easy as his cock slipped between her lips. "But I will pinch harder," she eventually said, pausing to shift his balls in the palm of her hand. "Your cock down my throat, my hand fondling your balls, and my fingers pinching my tits, what an evening. The only thing missing is a cock in my pussy and ass, or at least a toy in each, maybe your fingers." She watched him absorb her statement, but his next comment told her he was already past imagining.

"You'll make me come soon," he managed, his words more a groan than conversation. "But that was your point, so where, Kay? Are you going to swallow my cum or am I going to come on your tits?"

"On my tits," she told him and rose up on her knees, bringing her body closer. Kay took several long passes over his cock and pulled back, pumping him with one hand while directing his cock toward her nipples. With her other hand, she slid first one, then a second finger in his anus. His body reared up off the seat when he came, leaving long spurts of cum on her chest. Stuart dropped back into the seat, exhausted, and watched as she rubbed his cum across her tits.

Kay had accomplished what she set out to. She'd made him come and got him thinking about what else they might do together. She tugged her bra back in place and clasped it over her cum-coated breasts. Then she pulled her shirt back and buttoned it. Before standing, she leaned forward and took one last lap of Stuart's cock. "You think about what we've talked about, together and with Travis, and get back to me."

Kay stood and finished straightening her clothing. "I suppose I should have been more delicate about all this, but I've learned blunt works best most times. I could have danced around all this, but I'd rather we all know up front what our exceptions are so nobody gets hurt. And before you ask, I haven't mentioned this to Travis yet. I wanted to get your decision before suggesting this to him."

She wandered to the office door. "If you want to finish what I started there," she nodded to his crotch, his cock still exposed, "come by my room later." She opened the door and then hesitated. "I'm going to see Chloe for a bit. I'll be back at my apartment in a little while."

Kay left Stuart seemingly stunned into silence. As she walked to the old barn, she experienced a sense of pride she'd not felt in a long time, too long, she decided. She'd done the conventional route the first time, and now she wanted an arrangement that suited her needs, not some outdated societal rules.

Yes, she told herself, Stuart might run the other direction, but if he didn't, well, the possibilities were endless. Most of all, she'd be the lead in the group, if it happened. Never again would she take what was offered and accept it. From now on, she'd make happen what she wanted and hopefully have some fun along the way. She felt by being bold tonight, she'd laid the groundwork of what might turn into her complete sexual awakening.

Kay knew if Stuart didn't want this arrangement, she'd move on and eventually find a man who did. But deep inside, ever since she saw that damn photograph of him and Travis together, she'd wanted both men. Under her and in her in all ways. It would be interesting to see what developed.

Chapter Fifteen

Stuart sat behind his desk for a long time, his pants still open, his cock semi-hard just thinking about how she'd made him come. Now he had decisions to make. If he wanted to have an affair with her and he did, he could deal with her need for toys. Could he deal with having Travis or another man in bed with them? He shook his head at the whole situation, snorting back a laugh.

It wouldn't be the first time he and Travis shared a woman. When they first met playing baseball it was easy for them to share the women who hung around the team, almost felt natural. But that was a long time ago and neither man had any emotions invested in the women. Kay was different. Already he had feelings for her that made him uncomfortable. He knew Travis had a major crush on her and had been with her. But how would he feel sharing Kay?

At first he figured he'd just do it, and when it all blew up in their faces she'd move on. But after considering the situation further, after picturing her swallowing his cock and pinching her nipples, he wasn't sure he was man enough to allow any man to touch her in his presence. What he didn't know or see didn't hurt him. But could he live with the idea that when they weren't together, she might be with other men? It all came back to commitments, and that, he decided, was his point of contention.

"Damn that woman," he said aloud as he stood and straightened his pants. Old Harley jumped down from the sofa and was waiting beside the door when he finally decided to check on Chloe. Stuart knew meeting Kay in the barn would complicate their relationship. He let his hard-on decide for him.

At first glance, he saw her at the far end, leaning over the stall door, watching the dogs. He shut the main door behind him and made sure they were alone, checking each stall he passed. Her stance didn't change as he approached, and all he could think about was the way her butt was pushed backward, as if she were waiting for him to fondle her and fuck her.

"The pups are getting big so fast," she said in acknowledgement of his presence but not turning to look at him.

"That's what's supposed to happen." He moved behind her and dropped his arms on top of the stall door, bracketing her body against his.

"What's supposed to happen to us now?"

Stuart let his hands stroke her upper arms, and she didn't object. Without thinking before he acted, he reached around her and, with a side of her shirt in either hand, tugged until the material gave way and tore apart. He grasped her breasts, heavy in his hands, and started to pump his fingers around them. "Your nipples are hard," he told her as he sucked a patch of delicate skin behind her ear between his lips.

"And still coated in your cum."

"Is that a hint, Kay? Am I supposed to lick my cum from your tits?"

"I suppose it would be a start," she told him and raised her hand to unclasp her bra. It popped aside, letting him feel the heat of her skin as he tweaked her nipples. "Keep doing that and my nipples will be as hard as Chole's."

"But you don't have a pup to suckle each one."

Stuart wasn't prepared for her cynical laugh. "I could," she told him, laughing when he went to pull his hands from her. She lifted her hands and steadied his back on her tits before he could pull away. "Damn, I can't even joke with you."

"Now I've got a mental picture of me and…Travis, I suppose, each sucking one of your tits."

"What else do you see?"

"I think the more important question is what do you envision?" He continued to massage her breasts, her nipples hard against his calloused fingertips.

"Right about now, I'd like to feel your cock in my pussy, from behind."

"That's what you want, me fucking you from behind?" Stuart didn't hesitate his continued tweaking when she shifted in front of him and he realized she was unzipping her jeans. It was her hands that pushed them and a pair of blue silk panties down her thighs, and her body that moved back to push against his crotch.

"You're getting hard again. I can feel you against me."

"I can't imagine why," he said in a sarcastic tone. Stuart dropped his hands and unzipped his own pants, pausing only to pull a condom from his wallet before he snugged back against her butt. "Hold this," he told her and handed her the condom package. One hand went back to her breast while his other slid around her waist and snaked down to her crotch. His finger pressed between her pussy lips and found them full and damp. "Damn, you're hot and ready." He thrust his finger deeper and finally inside her pussy when she shifted her hips.

"That's a start," Kay said, rotating her hips to take his finger deeper. "I can feel your hard cock riding between my ass cheeks. It's getting harder."

"That's what's supposed to happen, isn't it?"

"God, I hope so. Don't tease me any longer, just fuck me."

"In my own time." He lightly bit the back of her neck and slid a second finger in her pussy. His other hand continued to pump her breast and twist her nipple.

"Your cock is so hard, Stuart. What will it take to get you inside me?"

"When I'm ready. I like teasing you, making you wait." He took his hand from her breast and stroked it against her mouth. She sucked it immediately. "Pinch your nipples, Kay." She lifted her hand without question and started to pull on one in rhythm with sucking his finger between her lips. Her other hand still grasped the condom package.

"Oh, baby, you are so hot," he whispered, pulling his fingers from her lips and dropping them to her ass. He took his cock in hand and began rubbing it up and down her butt crack while fingering her pussy. "You've got me ready to come already, Kay."

"Then do it, come on my ass, but you have to lick it off." Her silent dare wasn't lost on him.

"I'd rather lick it from your pussy," he managed, pulling completely away from her. He grabbed the condom from her and tore it open, sheathing himself. With his hands on her hips he pulled her backward a step, widening her stance as far as her puddled jeans around her ankles would let him. His cock was inside her wet, hot pussy in one push. He had to still or lose his composure, and he wanted to fuck her, long and slow, not just come inside her immediately.

"I'm so full," Kay said, pushing back to meet each thrust. "You're huge inside me, Stuart. Do you know how large your cock is? I knew when I first felt you this afternoon you'd be large, but sucking you down my throat was positive proof. I knew you'd stretch my pussy wide. Fuck me until I come."

"I'll fuck you until I come," he said, his fingers biting into her hips a bit harder. In the back of his mind he wanted to take this slow and make her beg for more. In reality, his dick did his thinking for him, and he was pumping in and out of her as fast as he could. "Damn you, Kay, you're so fucking tight, it's like you're milking me."

"That should be a good thing." Her tone was light and teasing. "Stuart, don't stop now, whatever you do, don't stop."

He interpreted her words as a plea and used all his might to push deeper.

Stuart knew he'd come soon. The signs were there, his mind losing control to his body. In one last moment of clarity, he pushed his thumb in her mouth, which she immediately started sucking like she had his cock earlier. He pulled it from between her lips and, without a verbal warning, slipped it between her ass cheeks and into her anus.

"Fuck me," she cried out, and for only a few strokes, he fucked both her holes until her body shuddering around him sucked his restraint and made him come. "Don't pull away," she cried, and he managed to hold himself in place.

While gasping for air, Stuart felt her inner muscles contracting around his cock and his finger. Her body spoke for her, the intensity and urgency building from inside out. He pulled his finger from her ass only halfway before pushing it back. Kay groaned her approval, and he did it again. He continued to finger-fuck her ass, feeling it against his cock, feeling himself come back to life inside her.

"That's it, that's what I need." She braced her hands on the stall door and pushed back against him. Her whole body shook when her orgasm hit, penetrating the movement to him. He felt himself come again, a small orgasm, but definitely an orgasm, and was astonished.

While he'd never need little blue pills to enhance his sex life, he usually needed downtime between orgasms. Tonight, in the barn, taking Kay against the stall door, he'd come twice. The first time was because she was so tight. But when she started humping him, he figured it was all for her. How wrong he was. Between her tight pussy and his finger stroking himself through her walls, he'd been harder than the first time. This orgasm was purely emotional on a new level. He hated her at that second, and himself for taking her. He knew better than to cross the line with her, but he'd gotten reckless, and now he was all emotional. Hell, he realized, he was holding her to him, his arm locked around her waist. If they were in bed, he'd be spooning her.

Gravity and Kay's juices eventually had his cock slipping from her body. Only then did he move his finger from her ass. Suddenly he was conscious of their surroundings, the sounds and smells of the barn. Glancing around, he was relieved nobody had come in during this episode. Now he had to figure out what to say. Thankfully, she spoke first.

"I had high hopes for you, Stuart, but I underestimated your stamina. I like it." She laughed and pulled from his grasp, taking a step to the side. He noted she bent provocatively to slide her undies and pants back up her legs.

"Stay like that and I'll fuck your ass."

"Right now," she winked at him, "I'm game if you're capable."

"Later, when I want to."

"Going to make me beg for your cock," she joked, and finally straightened up. She turned to face him while she tugged her bra back in place to cover her breasts. "My breasts are still needy, heavy." She tugged her nipples. "You never even sucked them." Laughing again, she pulled the shirt into place and tucked in the waist of her jeans, not bothering to attempt to button the few ones remaining after he tore it open.

Stuart held back a smile. "Next time," he told her and finally reached down, pulling his pants back up his hips. He paused and pulled off the condom before walking to the garbage pail two stalls down. He paused there and fastened his pants in place before turning to look at her.

"You are one amazing fuck, lady."

"Now you just have to decide what to do with me, how you think you're going to handle me." She said it with humor, but her words were accurate. "I'm going home to shower. I have to be up early." Kay walked forward, pausing to kiss his cheek, then turned on her heel and walked away, leaving him in the barn.

"Holy shit," he said aloud, running his fingers through his hair. "What the hell just happened? I thought I was supposed to be in control." The irony of the whole night wasn't lost on him. Kay had made her point. But that didn't wipe the smile off his lips on the walk back to the lodge.

Chapter Sixteen

Stuart made a point of staying out of the kitchen for a few days, needing time to think about his experience with Kay. Beyond all the reasons he knew they shouldn't get together, he realized he didn't want to share her. So it would be better not to have her at all. After the weekly Wednesday meeting he stalled outside the kitchen door, studying her garden, which was flourishing. It pissed him off just slightly that she hadn't failed. What did that say about him, he was wondering when she opened the back door.

"Got a minute for me?" she asked, her tone professional for those in the kitchen who might overhear.

"Yeah, walk with me to the kennels. I want to see how Chloe and the pups are adjusting." She fell in step beside him, but they didn't talk. When they were well away from prying ears and eyes he heard her pull a deep breath.

"You don't have to say anything, Stuart. Actions are louder than words. I understand you don't want a relationship with me and I accept it."

"What makes you think that was where this conversation was going?"

"I'm not a dolt." She laughed aloud. "I knew the night we…fucked so magnificently that you wouldn't continue. I suppose I could have been demure and accepting instead of demonstrative and asking for what I needed, but it's not my style anymore. From now on, I'll speak what's on my mind. It's the only way I get satisfied. I won't apologize for being bold."

"It's just that it's not smart business to be sleeping with my chef."

"That was a slip, Stuart. I'm your pastry chef, and Travis is your chef. That's what you can't get past, my wanting both of you. It makes me wonder if it's because you're afraid of your feelings for Travis? I've heard bits about your early days in the baseball league together, how you shared women then. But something stopped that. I assumed it was because your circumstances changed and the groupies weren't around. Now I wonder if it was because you were afraid of restarting that side of your relationship with Travis."

They were still walking, but his step faltered. She nodded at him. Stuart knew she was baiting him just for her pleasure to watch him squirm. "Did the two of you ever touch each other, maybe suck each other's cocks or occasionally fuck one another?" He stopped dead and glared at her. She didn't hold back her sly smile. "Have I gone too far, asking if you two ever fucked? I haven't asked Travis. Would he tell me the truth? It doesn't matter. It would be interesting to watch, I think, how you two would touch. It would be better to center all your attention on me and ravish my body." He still stood rooted to the spot, looking at her with a blind stare. "Either way I've hit a sore spot…you'd never tell me the truth now anyway."

Finally, he started grumbling under his breath and headed for the kennels. He figured she could only make out a few curse words walking beside him, but it was enough to let her know she'd pushed a button. He was debating if she'd gone too far this time. "But I have to accept your decision, so I won't be a problem. I won't come taunting you at inappropriate times. I'll just take our time as a memory."

They were halfway to the kennels when she paused. "Does that about cover the conversation?"

"Yes, I suppose so. I thought…"

"That I'd fight or get nasty or clingy? Not my style anymore. I had a good time with you. I'd rather just keep that memory."

"I'm relieved you understand, but somehow I'm disappointed. I feel like I'm being challenged and dismissed at the same time. You're an interesting woman, Kay, in many ways."

“Not dismissed, really. Just gracefully let go.” Kay reached to his cheek and ran her fingers through his beard. “It is a shame I never got to feel your beard between my thighs, but I accept your decision. I hope you find someone that fills your sex needs.”

“Maybe you should just go back to Travis full time.”

“Travis and I will never be full-time or permanent. We’ve found our level of friendship and sex that works for both of us. I do have one question though. Do you feel it would make you gay or bisexual to have another man in bed with us?”

He smiled at her, finally relaxing. “No, Travis and I shared women in our younger days. There was never a jealousy problem or unanswered or unexplored feelings between us.”

“So I’m the problem. You don’t want to share me. Thank you, Stuart, that means a lot whether you realize it or not.” Kay turned and wandered away from him slowly, not turning back once. He went on to the kennels and spent some time with the dogs, trying to figure out how his life got so complicated.

Petting Chloe, he spoke to the dog as if she could understand. “I guess I just wasn’t enough for her.” The dog looked at him and blinked. “Maybe she was right. It took all I had to satisfy her for one evening. I don’t think I have the stamina to do her on a continuing basis. I’d die of exhaustion.” He put the dog down and shook off his maudlin thoughts. Travis would be a better fit to her libido. Maybe it was time for him to spend some time away from the lodge. Find a woman who wasn’t always within arm’s reach, one who would be thankful just to have him to herself.

* * * *

Summer was in full swing. Travis was grumbling about the fishermen and their catch, wanting to serve wonderful steaks and barbeque. The guests wanted to eat what they caught. Kay was on a short fuse, too. The heat had finally gotten to her, as well as the tension between her and Stuart. Kay knew the night she told him about his photograph being the draw for her to accept the job at the lodge she'd lost him. She'd felt him shut down, physically and emotionally, when he told her he didn't want to continue a relationship with her. For the weeks that had gone by, they'd seen very little of each other.

Kay did her job to the best of her ability and spent almost all of her downtime in town with Grace and Lisa. After the Timms incident, she and Lisa had begun to form a tentative friendship, one they included Grace in. The three of them were an odd mix, yet they complemented one another. Neither Kay nor Lisa ever mentioned Stuart or his short temper when they were away from work. It was an unspoken rule between them and it extended to Travis, too.

The construction on Stuart's home had begun, large boring machines having been brought in to sink the pilings his raised structure would be built on. She'd seen the site from the distance when she ran but never went close enough to investigate further.

Chloe was back in the second pen, and her puppies were all spoken for. Over the next two weeks, all of them would go to good homes, and while it was a relief, it was also extremely sad.

Only on Wednesday afternoons did Kay and Stuart force themselves to spend time in the same space. Their weekly manager's meeting was an ordeal they both managed to get through, but just barely. Hoyt had mentioned the status of Kay's garden last week, and she saw the muscle over Stuart's left eye contract. Holding back a grin, Kay wouldn't admit it was more work than she'd imagined. Instead, she suffered in the heat and mosquitoes in silence to keep it a showplace that no one would dare degrade. She longed for an early frost so she could finally let it go to seed. She knew there was a long time to go before then and prayed she'd have the strength to maintain it. Only remembering Stuart's first words on the subject kept her focused. She'd not give him the satisfaction of abandoning it. Deep down, she figured he was enjoying her discomfort.

Hoyt had given Kay a few quick riding lessons, but only when Stuart was off site. Never did she allow him to see her tentative movements with the horse, even though the mount she'd been given was docile and trained. Just the height took adjusting to, let alone straddling the beast and letting him carry her down the path. Hoyt had joked with her that she was a woman who liked being grounded, and she'd agreed. With each lesson she'd become more at ease, but wouldn't consider horseback riding as a sport or enjoyment just yet. She decided she was forcing herself to learn to annoy Stuart and it worked for her. Just like the garden, she refused to let him see her struggle.

* * * *

Stuart had kept himself beyond busy. With the construction on his home starting and the lodge being booked solid, he was on the go all the time. He'd managed to find a replacement for Jimmy Timms but kept a tight eye on the marina and its new manager. While it was only weeks since his day with Kay, he felt a lifetime older. And every time he walked past Kay's garden, his stomach tightened. He'd caught glimpses of her working in it almost daily and wondered if she was keeping it up just to annoy him. He'd decided she was and knew if the positions were reversed, he'd do the same thing.

What he didn't need now was the tropical storm working its way north. If it stayed a storm, it would be a major inconvenience. If it turned into a hurricane, it would be a horror. But like anyone who lived on the coast, it was a reality that had to be dealt with.

Tuesday afternoon, he called the managers together for a quick meeting. Everyone was given the storm plan, and last-minute decisions were made. The dogs would be moved to the barn, and all the boats would be pulled from the water. The generators were checked as well as their fuel supplies. Kay and Travis made up menus of prepare-ahead meals, as well as taking into account the lodge-bound guests who would expect the first-class service of the lodge to continue even if there was a storm.

Wednesday night, the storm strengthened as it hit the coast of Florida. Thankfully, it petered out and raced up the coast as a windy day that was inconvenient but not destructive. By Thursday night, all of Agrarian Lodge was back in top working order. The guests had been only slightly inconvenienced, and life seemed to get back to a strained normal for Stuart and Kay.

* * * *

She'd thought long and hard in the last months and knew when her contract was up she'd move on. Where, she had no idea yet. Not back to New York, but definitely not any farther south either. She'd taken to doing a lot of research on the Internet and was planning her week's vacation for the Seattle area.

Travis and Lisa seemed to be bonding a tentative relationship but rarely acknowledged each other while at work. Kay didn't know how they spent their off time, but she knew Lisa was spending less time with her and Grace. Even Grace, dear, sweet, broken-hearted Grace, had started dating the basketball coach-math teacher from the local high school. Divorced with two teenage sons, he seemed to complement Grace's quiet presence with humor. Kay had accepted a blind date with one of his friends but only once. The commercial fisherman they set her up with had more arms than an octopus, and she didn't want to spend another night batting at his hands. It all brought back shades of Timms and made her uncomfortable. Instead, she took to spending time with Grace when she could and spending a lot more time alone with her research. She was also spending a lot of time in the kitchen at night.

It would be a sin to waste the crop of plum tomatoes just because she wasn't in the mood to deal with them. Sunday night, with the radio playing to keep her company, the smell of roasted garlic and olive oil wafted through the lodge. She'd been simmering the sauce down for hours and had just started pulling out the glass jars to store it in when Stuart entered her space. They looked at each other for a long time without saying a word. Kay took a small dish and filled it with the hot, spicy tomato sauce and placed it on the counter before him.

"There's fresh bread in the pantry," she told him, then went back to work. She refused to let him make her nervous and forced her hands to steady as she filled the jars.

"That's excellent, Kay. Is it the bounty from your garden?"

"Yes," she managed, before turning away from him. She dried her hands on a cloth and tossed it on the counter, leaving him in the space while she made a pretense of looking for something in the storage room. Hoping he'd be gone by the time she came out with a roll of labels in her hand, she watched him stare at her. "What?"

"I miss you," was all he said before walking from the room.

Kay leaned against the stainless steel counter and drank in his words. The idea that he was as miserable as she was made her feel better. It was stupid to think that way, but she did, misery loving company and all that. Somehow her task wasn't so trying anymore, and she sang with the radio as she finished. Only after the kitchen was cleaned and shut down did she hesitate.

The light was on in his office, the thin line of light coming from under his door, reflecting on the polished oak flooring. She didn't think, just acted. Her hand raised at the wood surface, she moved it to connect before she could turn away. Hearing his famous "In" was enough to make her palms sweaty. Opening the door, she found him at his desk, his head bent over the papers in front of him.

"I miss you, too," she said, waiting for him to acknowledge her presence. For a long time they watched each other, and finally she said, "It doesn't make a difference, does it?"

Stuart pushed back in his chair and studied her. His single-word answer of "No," was all she heard.

Kay didn't know if he said anything else, for she'd pulled the door shut behind her and walked back to her apartment. She wanted to cry but didn't. She wanted to sleep but couldn't. Even masturbating didn't give her the same level of satisfaction it used to, with or without toys. It was all so mechanical now.

In the early morning hours just as dawn approached, she let herself into the barn and carefully saddled her horse as Hoyt had taught her. Her ride to the beach had been uneventful, the horse taking her for a lazy ride.

That was how Stuart found her, sitting tall on the horse's back, her head toward the sky, her eyes shielded from the morning light by a baseball cap, her braided hair tugged through the back. He approached almost silently for a man on a horse and was beside her before she had time to react.

"Hoyt?" he asked. Kay only nodded he was correct. He glanced at the saddle and seemed pleasantly surprised to see it was correctly used. He watched her for a long time before asking, "Have you been to my home site lately?"

"No, it wouldn't be right for me to invade your private space." She turned the horse around and slowly let the beast take her from his side. When the horse was back in his stall and all the equipment stored properly, she took her time taking care of him before heading back to her apartment. Stuart didn't join her, and she was long showered and gone for the day by the time she saw him take his mount back to the stable. And that was how they spent the rest of the summer, avoiding each other at all costs.

* * * *

In September, both Travis and Lisa took their vacations the same week, leaving both Stuart and Kay busy covering their absences. Thankfully, the lodge was full, but the guest houses weren't rented that week. By the time Sunday afternoon rolled around, Kay was glad to see the backs of their guests. She'd had enough. Skipping supper with the rest of the crew, she was swimming laps in the deserted lodge when Stuart appeared. He watched her slide through the water and didn't turn away. Only after she stopped at the side of the pool and pulled herself out of the water did she acknowledge his presence.

"Stuart?" He didn't pretend not to watch her. Instead his eyes followed every movement of the plush towel that stroked over her wet limbs. Kay hadn't felt that self-conscious since she was a kid and pulled on a toweling robe to cover the clinging material that hugged every curve of her body. When she was covered he pulled himself from his appraisal of her.

"We have a problem," he started, and watched her stiffen.

"What is it?"

"Hurricane…" was all he managed to get out.

"When?" she asked, finger combing her wet hair. Kay folded the used towel and dropped it on the lounge chair she stood beside. Stuart seemed to stare at her and didn't answer for the longest time, during which Kay decided to watch him back. He seemed tired to her, the dark circles under his eyes reminiscent of the ones she bared. "When is it due to hit?"

"Mid-week," he said, rousing himself to her question.

"What needs to be done? What are they predicting for its path? What category do they think…Stuart?" Whatever he might have said was lost. Instead, he moved quickly toward her and pulled her to him.

"Damn it, Kay," he whispered, just before he kissed her. Stiff in his arms, he didn't release her from his hold until she softened under him, accepting his lips against hers. Arms threaded up around his shoulders as she opened her mouth under his, accepting his kiss before taking from him. Kay had a passing thought of pushing him away and didn't. She pressed her body along his, feeling his erection against her even through the heavy robe. His kiss left her weak against him, like he drew the life from her each time his tongue swept against hers. It was a heady experience, nothing like the few kisses they'd shared earlier in the summer. From Stuart, it was a form of lovemaking, not just a precursor to the act, she realized.

His hands slid the belt on her robe open and slipped along her waist. He didn't seem to care that she still wore the wet bathing suit; somehow it seemed to spur him on. His lips dropped to her chin and traced a line of kisses along her throat. Arching back, she allowed him more access as her fingers clutched at his shoulders. Kay felt the warmth spread through her and couldn't stifle a groan that forced its way through her. Her hips moved rhythmically against him, driving them deeper into the darkness he was creating. There was nobody to interrupt them.

Stuart pulled back from her and dropped onto the lounge, his head cradled in his hands. "I'm sorry, Kay."

"I'm not, Stuart," she told him with a half laugh.

"I'll leave you alone," he said in the most defeated voice she'd ever heard.

"You do that, Stu. You had your little fix, now walk away again for a few weeks." Kay wasn't sure where her attitude came from. All the lust and want she'd felt were churning inside her. She wanted the completion to what he'd started and wondered if she should push the issue. Instead, she simply walked from the pool area, forcing herself to keep her head up.

Chapter Seventeen

The storm came in as a category two and hesitated over the South Carolina coast for a full day. That left the North Carolina coast on the fringes, but not out of the path. While everyone had gathered in the lodge, Kay was restless. She managed to sneak away and made it to the barn without being noticed. All the animals seemed restless from the storm, too. The dogs were all corralled in a far stall, and the horses were on edge. Wet from her walk, she tugged off the rain slicker she'd pulled on over jeans and a T-shirt and tossed her umbrella aside. Her hair was wet and plastered to her face and neck, the wind taking her hood off several times during her trek.

Stroking the horses' noses as she passed, she uttered kind words to each animal and spent a few minutes at each stall, treating them to chunks of carrots and apples. When she got to the dogs they all started to bark. One word and they settled down. It was then she realized she wasn't alone.

"I thought you were in the office," she told him, defending her right to be in the barn.

"I was, until I saw you running in the storm."

"I'm fine," she started but couldn't finish her statement. He was as wet and seemed as miserable as she was.

"No, you're not, and neither am I, Kay." Studying her for a long time, he simply opened his arms to her.

Kay stood her ground, not running to him like she'd wanted to. Instead, she took a breath and spoke the words she knew would send him away.

"Stuart, I think you should know, I'm not going to be renewing my contract. Come January, I'll be moving on." She watched his arms drop to his sides, and he moved to lean on a stall door.

"Where?"

"Probably Seattle. I'm going there on my vacation at the end of the month. If not there, somewhere near there."

"Getting as far away from me as possible, Kay?"

"Something like that," she admitted. "You don't want me, Stuart, and being here only antagonizes us both. I thought you'd be happy to hear I'm going. You can go back to your no-emotions program and not have to worry that I'm stalking you." She let out a laugh, and it turned into a sob. Turning away, she moved quickly to the far end of the barn. She was struggling to put on her rain slicker when he met her, pulling her to face him.

"Is that what you really want?"

"No, it's what you want." Kay stood her ground and gave him a hard look.

"It's not what I want, Kay, and you know it." He released his grip on her arm and turned away from her.

"Isn't it? How else would I know, Stuart? I mean, you're such a talkative man, always clearly communicating your needs and feelings."

He spun around to defend himself and stopped short. Kay realized there was nothing he could say. She was right.

Somehow his defeated stance made her laugh. And her laugh got stronger and bolder as the seconds ticked by. Even though she knew he was smoldering with anger, she couldn't stop.

"You don't know what you want, Stuart. First you push me away, then you pull me back. It's a sick game I won't play any longer. We're not kids testing the ways of the world. I'm a woman who knows what she wants, and you're a man who can't give it to me. It's best I move on at the first of the year. At least then I'll find some peace."

Kay stared at him and waited for him to say something, anything.

When he didn't she had her answer. "Stuart, I'm sorry. I didn't come here to make your life miserable, only to try and find a new one for myself. You don't want any part of me or what I might bring to you, so it's the only option I have. I still have my one point of contention that you won't accept. Since I'm not married I want my freedom to occasionally bring another man into my sex life. You can't handle that. I get it. It takes a stronger man to understand that my needs come first to me now. I spent too many years doing what society told me was standard. I'm not a standard woman any longer. I'm willing to wait until I find men who aren't threatened by my sexuality and needs."

"What does Travis have to say about this?"

"Nothing. I've never mentioned the sex part to him seriously. I don't think I'd have to harass him for his attentions, temporary as they are. I haven't told him about my future yet. My contract reads through the first of the year with a three-month notice period on either side. I'll talk to him when I get back from vacation. I'll have a better idea of my plans after that. Until then, I figured you'd be relieved to know my days are numbered here."

"What would it take to make you stay?"

"Stay? Are you kidding me?" Kay tossed her rain jacket aside and stormed toward him. "Stay! You must be crazy. After the last six months of this sick game of *I want you, then I don't*? Why would I stay?"

"Because you care about me."

"Yes, I do, and you make it so easy to love you, Stuart." Kay took a step back and turned away. "Is that the problem, I didn't fight hard enough for you? Was I supposed to smother you with my attentions, only to be pushed away like a child who didn't know her place?"

All the emotions she'd kept at bay for so long surfaced. Even the animals around them had gone quiet, sensing the storm inside the barn was worse than the one raging outside.

"We're adults, Stuart. I want a man, not a boy hiding in a man's body, afraid to make a commitment to anything that has a brain and can think for itself or works outside the norm. No wonder you're so good with animals—they understand their place with you. Only when you're in the mood for them. Otherwise, you leave them locked away in gilded cages and stables. I'm not a damn horse or a dog, Stuart. I want a man full time, not a half child afraid to confront his demons. I want him to be sure of his own masculinity to enjoy me and an occasional diversion."

Somehow she sensed she'd gone too far and tried to rein back her temper. Kay saw the vein in his temple throb, and she turned away. "Would you prefer I find a replacement? I won't keep you to the contract." Again he had no answer, and she reeled back to him.

"Damn it, Stuart, talk to me. I can't read your mind. You kiss me with a passion I've never experienced before, yet you pull away when I react." Staring him down once more, she shook her head at him, a weary smile crossing her lips. "Thanks for letting me vent," she told him, this time managing to make it to the door before he spoke.

"Kay, don't leave." He said the words aloud and seemed confused he had.

"Don't leave now, as in this moment or as in don't leave the lodge?"

"Both."

"Why, Stuart? Tell me why I should stay?"

"Because I've fallen in love with you."

Kay watched his face and understood he surprised himself as much as her.

"You don't love me. If you did, you wouldn't treat me the way you do. Maybe you lust after me, but we both know once your itch is scratched, you'll want nothing more to do with me."

"That's one possibility, I admit. The other is that once we're together for more than a quick fuck, I can't go back to the life I had."

"So it's better that I move on then. This is your home, your land, and your business. I never wanted to make you uncomfortable in your own space, but that's exactly what happened. By being honest from the start, I ruined any chance we might have had, even just for some fun. But I still felt it better to be truthful than surprise you with my wants and needs a few months in."

"You've made me uncomfortable since I first heard about you from Travis," he said, his laugh tentative.

Kay watched him, speechless. She knew they could have some fun in the barn one last time, but it wasn't what she wanted. The old adage came back to her: Be careful what you wish for, or you just might get it. If he touched her now, he'd be imprinted on her permanently. Ultimately, she'd still have to leave him. The irony of their situation wasn't lost on her. She'd believed in fidelity all her life until her marriage. Now she wanted to draft the standards of her life on her terms. It would be easy to tell him what he needed to hear, that he'd be the only one she'd sleep with. But Kay knew that would be an outright lie. Better to disappoint him now than to hurt him later when she wanted more and he couldn't accept her want.

"If I touch you, Kay, it will be forever. Can you honestly tell me that you'd stay with me forever? That you'd stay with just me?"

"I don't know. I don't know you well enough. Probably not. You're not open enough with your feelings, and it drives me crazy. I already had one marriage to a man who couldn't commit. I don't want another…relationship I have to second-guess every day. Worse yet, you'd never trust me. You'd always wonder if I was doing another man when we weren't together or was wishing for more."

"What do you want in a relationship? Because you chose to ignore the word *husband*."

"I want my man to love me unconditionally. Good and bad alike. I want him to need me as much as I need him. And he needs to understand…"

Stuart moved closer to her, and her words died away. He stopped within inches of her, the humid air between them thick.

"Understand what? That you were hurt once, or that he has to be a puppet you can control? That's what it comes down to, isn't it? You want a man you can control. One you can predict each response from and never worry he might have a stray thought you didn't put in his mind. One who will share you when you're so inclined."

"No, I want a man who stands up for himself and for me, no matter what."

"And what will you give this man, Kay? What's his reward for surrendering his being to you?"

"If he loved me, he wouldn't feel like he was losing anything. Instead, he'd be gaining a partner, someone he can count on without question."

"Take off your rose-colored glasses, Kay. Real life doesn't exist that way."

"As if you live in the real world. You hide away on this acreage so the world can't find you, figuring you can't be hurt again. You don't want a partner or wife, Stuart, you want a mistress that comes to you when you're in the mood and disappears into the recess of your life when it's inconvenient." Pausing for air, she finished with, "I'm not the sidelines kind of woman. I'll be inconvenient and noisy, pushy and demanding when you don't live up to my expectations."

"Let's look at this from a different perspective, one we haven't discussed. One you haven't thought of."

"So what am I missing?" She turned to watch him, wanting to understand his perspective.

"You want a monogamous relationship with permission to bring another man into the bedroom occasionally. What if I wanted to bring another woman into the bedroom with us? How would you feel about that?"

Her outright laugh wasn't what he was expecting from the grimace on his face. "I've been there and done that. Women don't have the right equipment to satisfy me long term, but they are very sensual creatures. I enjoyed my experiences and wouldn't change them, I'm just not looking for a pussy to lick. I like sucking men's cocks, having a live cock inside me, not plastic replicas."

She laughed harder. "Was I supposed to be outraged by your thought? I'm not, I just know myself and my needs. I've come a long way in the past years, come to terms with more than you can imagine. I like men, I only have sex with men. Nothing against women, but most times, they're just too emotional in the long run."

He seemed stunned by her admission, and she held back her smile. She'd assumed he'd bring up this counterpoint long ago and was prepared with her answer. "You see, I'm not the sheltered woman you think I am or apparently need me to be. Life is messy in all directions. We all have to decide what works for us. Men work for me." She hesitated but added, "What about a woman with a cock? That might have its possibilities." Kay didn't hold back her smirk, knowing she'd topped him again.

"That sounds like a dare," he teased, trying to settle them both down.

"No, it's a promise. I understand who I am and what pleasures me. Somewhere out there are a few men who can satisfy my needs and theirs without all the drama. It's just sex I want the other man for, not emotions or partnership. Just all out fucking. I want…"

His hand reached to her chin, his fingers tilting it to see her. "What do you want, Kay?" he asked again, just before his lips covered hers. When he pulled back, her eyes were closed, and it was several seconds before she opened them.

"I want you, Stuart, I want the man you hide inside. I want the full-fledged male that you're afraid to let loose." Her answer was barely a whisper, and she waited for his response.

"He doesn't exist, Kay. You saw a picture and made me the dream man you wished you'd married the first time. Only I'm not him. I have faults and fears just like you."

"You do exist," she managed, just before she boldly took his face between her hands, her fingers running through his beard lightly, teasing the skin underneath.

"Not the way you think," he groaned just before he lifted her up against the length of his body and moved to the first empty stall. Stuart literally dropped her onto the fresh bedding of straw before kneeling down beside her. His movements were harsh, his large hands pulling the neckline of her shirt until it tore in two. With a tug, the rest of her shirt fell away.

Kay took in a swift breath at his actions but didn't pull away. Instead, she reached to him and took his hands. Placing them on her lace-covered breasts, he shut his eyes as he closed his fingers over her. Kay worked hers at his belt, fighting to free him. She cursed loudly and pulled away from him, only to have him push her back down. Stuart flipped open the small plastic clasp on her bra and sat back on his heels as she was bared to him.

"God, Kay, you're so beautiful," he whispered just before his mouth covered first one breast, then the other. She let her body go with his hands and his lips, her fingers closing around the straw she lay on. He was on top of her, and his hand on her stomach felt hot and heavy as he traced his way down to her jeans. Without taking his lips from her breast, he managed to open the zipper and slipped his hand against her, finding her hot and melting for him.

"Damn it, Kay," he whispered just before he kissed her again. This time when her hands went to his belt, he didn't push her away. He groaned around her nipple when her hand found his erect cock. Her fingers teased him and finally she slipped them under the band of his underwear, taking him in her palm, feeling his strength and desire. Kay encased him with her fingers and matched the strokes of his tongue against her skin. His hand slipped under the lace of her panties. It was too much not to arch toward him, and finally he teased her slick folds, his index finger slipping inside her. Stuart moved back to her breast and slipped a second finger inside her. Kay moved with him as her hand moved on him.

"Stuart, please, come inside me."

"Later, Kay. I've dreamed about you for months now," he told her before he took her for another ride with his kiss. She felt him surge in her palm and tensed when he pulled from her.

* * * *

Efficiently he stripped her jeans and panties down her legs, stopping only to pull off her boots. Tossing them aside, he finished pulling off her pants. With Kay lying spread before him in the stall, the winds from the storm howling outside, Stuart knew the moment was beyond surreal.

He let himself drop between her legs and pulled her up to him, giving her the intimate kiss he'd longed for. He took his time when he knew she wanted fast and hard. He teased her until she relaxed under him, understanding he was in charge for the moment. His lips and tongue brought her to a crest; his fingers replaced inside her pushed her over the edge. He heard her groan and felt her body tighten over his fingers.

"You're so wet," he told her, sliding his fingers in and out of her pussy. It amazed him that she let her body ride him so easily without embarrassment, taking what he gave and pushing him for more. His other hand rose to her breast and pumped her tit in unison with his other hand.

"Damn it, you're so tight," he told her and grasped her thighs, bringing her legs up over his shoulders. This position left his mouth directly at her pussy, and he tongued her lips, pausing occasionally to suck her clit. She shifted under him, silently asking for more. With a slight adjustment, he was able to lick her pussy and anus in one long swipe of his tongue. That had her writhing at his touch.

Stuart knew he'd come in his jeans if he didn't stop soon. He felt his cock harden further and knew droplets of cum were being released of their own accord.

Stuart continued his onslaught, accepting her subtle shifts to deepen his movements. He left her legs resting on his shoulders and slid one finger in her pussy again, then a second. Kay cried out in anguish when he pulled his hand completely from her body. She groaned in approval when he slid his middle finger in her anus, fucking her gently with the digit until her words penetrated his brain.

"That's it, Stuart, fuck my ass, let me feel you fuck me, stretch me wide so your cock will fit." She'd opened her eyes and stared at him, almost a dare, he decided.

"That's what you want, me to fuck your ass?"

"Eventually," she whispered, accepting a second finger. "First, make me come with your fingers, then your cock."

"You truly do know what you want," he said, more to himself than her, but he realized it was rare for a woman to actually tell him directly what she wanted.

He didn't question her further, didn't reinforce her directions. His cock throbbed harder, and he figured it was time for his release. Stuart took his fingers from her body and let her legs drop to the floor. He rose up over her and tugged down his own jeans, stopping to find his wallet and pull out the sealed protection he'd put there months before. Stuart dropped back and knelt between her legs, finally pulling her by the hips to meet his cock. Tugging her legs up over his hips, he quickly filled her pussy in one smooth stroke, burying himself until he was deeply embedded. Then he let himself take a breath. Glancing at her, he saw her eyes were closed, her head thrown back, her hands grasping at the straw.

"Look at me, Kadence," he said as he moved slightly from her. He pushed back only after she opened her eyes.

"Please, Stuart," she said, her hands finding his hips and pulling him closer to him. When he moved inside her without moving over her she groaned a low "Yes," before her eyes closed again. Having regained a bit of his control, he proceeded to love her with an intensity he hadn't known existed within him. A light layer of sweat coated them both as he moved above her and inside her, his fingers tempting her nipples to buds. He decided to take his time, knowing she wanted quick. This time, he'd fuck her with his own need first. If he continued this pace, he knew he'd come, and he wanted this to last.

* * * *

Kay wanted more, needed the release he'd started within her now, not later. On that thought, she managed to push his hands from her breasts and took a deep breath. Startled at being pushed away, he let her roll him onto his back as she straddled him. That was what Kay had wanted, control of him inside her.

Staring down at him, she had a strange smile on her lips. Kay knew he could feel her inner movements while she made no movement above him. She milked him with her inner muscles, a delicious test of his staying ability. When she neared her peak, she dropped her head back on her shoulders and took his hands in hers, placing them over her breasts. That was when she rode him with long strokes and short ones alike, changing the rhythm and pattern just when he'd catch up. She dropped over his chest, keeping him deeply embedded inside, and took his mouth, took him into a darkness she created above him, and pushed them both into the abyss.

Kay felt him tense under her and finally collapse. She managed to stay above him but braced herself against his waist. Stuart's hands came up to her waist to hold her in place, his eyes watching her intently. Neither said a word; only Kay started her inner movements again, bringing him to fullness a second time. Stuart watched her definite movements and the concentration on her face. She wanted to change positions but was afraid if she moved, it would end.

"What do you want this time?" she asked, twitching her hips over him.

"Now I get a say," he teased.

She flexed her inner muscles around him and again brought his hands to her breasts, pushing them against her skin.

"Tell me what you want," she managed, tossing her head back to change the position of his cock within her walls. Stuart rolled her under him quickly in a missionary position. His thrusts became more pronounced, more intense with each stroke. But Kay wanted more. She figured if this was one last fuck, she'd experience him fully. Her fingers braced on his hips on an outward move, and she got his attention. He let her slide out from under him and immediately pushed back in her pussy as soon as she turned over and rose to her knees. With her weight planted on her hands in front of her, she offered her ass for his taking. Kay heard him breathing heavily, almost growling behind her as his fingers bit into her hips and pulled her onto his cock, filling her pussy from a new angle.

"That's better, you're deeper in me this way." Kay glanced over her shoulder and smiled at him. "Take me, Stuart, the way you want to. I'm not fragile, I won't break. Fuck me the way you need to." He moved deeper in her pussy, exerting a deeper force within her. She accepted his not quite punishing movements, arching backward when he hesitated, his breathing uneven. Kay turned back to stare at him and smiled, whispering only, "More," before she turned away and wiggled over him. "Fuck my ass, Stuart, fill me with your cock and push your fingers in my pussy."

There was no conversation. He simply pulled from her pussy and thrust higher, taking her anus in one smooth push. He stalled a bit, but she waited him out, knowing he was probably trying not to come.

"Push your own finger in your pussy," he told her, and she eagerly complied.

Stuart let himself go, forgot to keep his mind and body in check, and fucked her with full abandon. When he felt her go slick around him a second time, he let himself have the release he was straining to hold back. With his final thrust, he dropped over her, managing to take some of his weight onto his arms.

"Damn it, Kay," he said, but it took all his effort to manage that.

"More," she said, and watched him lift off her enough to see her face.

With a wide smile, he shook his head at her. "More?" he asked, unsure he heard her correctly, and she laughed at him.

"Yes, do it again, Stuart." Her hand reached to his shoulders and pulled him down to her mouth. It was a long, slow, lazy kiss that had them both starting up the climb toward fulfillment once again when the winds outside changed. They both realized the difference, and he pulled sharply back from her.

"Get dressed, Kay," he told her harshly. Stuart pulled from inside her with a fury that annoyed her until she realized he was aware of something she wasn't. Looking around, she realized the power had gone off and the stable roof was heaving.

Pulling up his jeans, Stuart struggled to right himself inside them. Then he pulled off his flannel shirt and wrapped it around her shoulders. Buttoning it in place, she too hurried to pull on her jeans and boots. He reached a hand down to her to help her up, and while she would have liked to stay in his arms to enjoy the afterglow, she understood it wasn't to be.

"Stay here, I'm going to check…"

"I'm going with you," she said, tugging his shirt down over her as she rolled back the long sleeves.

"Damn it, Kay, can't you just once do what I ask?"

"Damn it, Kay," she mimicked. "Stuart, you say it like my name is Damn it Kay." For about five seconds they stared each other down, and he finally smiled at her.

"All right, but stay close," he told her, and she accepted his statement with a nod.

They moved to the front door closest to the lodge, and both had to hold it from snapping in the wind. Torrents of rain splashed them, and the wind whipped at their faces. "The storm moved," he started. "Kay, check the horses. Make sure their doors are secure."

He moved to one side of the row, and she took the opposite, checking each stall and its occupant. When he reached the dogs he went in and soothed them for a few minutes.

"I have to get back to the lodge. I want you to stay here. You'll be safe and dry…"

"I'm coming with you," she told him as she pulled on her rain jacket. He gave her his look that meant he was about to argue with her when she leaned up and gave him a wet, sloppy kiss on the lips. "Discussion over. If you go alone, you'll want to come back for me. This way we'll only be outside once, together."

It was obvious he didn't like her second-guessing him, but accepted the validity of her words.

"Okay, but stay close. I don't think taking the truck…"

"I walked over in the first place. I won't melt in the rain." Her look dared him to suggest otherwise.

"And what are you going to tell everyone you were doing in the barn with me?" he asked, pulling a few small strands of straw from her hair. "For the last three hours?"

"Do you really think they need to ask?" She laughed openly at him, and he nodded she was right. "Just about every person who works at Agrarian Lodge knows the tension between us." She hesitated and waited for him to argue. "Besides, I'm wearing your shirt and your scent," she told him.

"Oh, hell, Kay, do you mind?" he asked, his voice tender with concern.

"No, do you? As far as I'm concerned, I don't care what they think, only what you think." He studied her for a long time, and she added, "I could go to my apartment and clean up and meet you back at the lodge if you'll feel better. Nobody would have to know…"

"I only care about you, Kay."

Chapter Eighteen

Kay was thankful the storm had passed without much damage. The last few days were filled with setting the lodge to rights and getting everything back in working order. By Sunday night, she was appreciative all was quiet. They had the next day to themselves and by Tuesday, a new round of guests would arrive, along with all the chaos they brought. Tonight, she just wanted to relax.

Fresh from the shower she cussed at the knocking on her apartment door. Tucking the towel wrapped around her torso tighter, she flung the door inward, full of attitude.

“What?” She wasn’t prepared for Travis to be standing there with a bottle of scotch in one hand.

“We’ve been summoned to the office,” he said, pausing to twist open the top and take a drink. He handed it to her and she took a sip too. “Don’t know what it’s about, but I figured since it’s our evening off, we have the right to a drink.”

“I’ll need a few minutes to dry and dress.” Handing him back the bottle, she eyed him up and down. “You look sexy tonight, Travis, like you’re primed for something. Want to share?”

“No ideas, I was relaxing and having a drink when Stuart called. I told him I’d pick you up on the way over.”

“So the glassy eyes are from alcohol?” She reached up and unwound the towel from her hair, blotting the excess moisture from the ends. “Want to come in and wait while I get dressed?”

“I think I’ll walk over and meet you there.” He gave her a look from head to toe. “Too much temptation here.” Travis took a step into her apartment and wrapped her wet hair between his fingers. His kiss was just short of rough, transferring heat and passion and need. When he released her, he took a step back and shifted his cock in his jeans. "I better walk slow to get rid of my hard-on." He laughed at his own words and disappeared from her doorway.

"Great, he's drunk and horny, and now he's made me horny, and I have to go sit with Stuart and listen to his garbage." Kay closed the door and headed back to her bathroom. After covering her body in lotion, she pulled on clean jeans and her clogs. She stood before the bureau, a front-close bra in her hands, deciding if she wanted to wear it or not. With a resigned laugh, she struggled into the torture device and settled her tits in the cups, clasping it tight. She pulled a white tee from the top of the pile and headed back to dry her hair.

Kay heard the knock and yelled, "Come in," but kept the hair dryer flowing underneath her hair. When she finally clicked it off and turned she let out an involuntary yell when she realized it was Timms standing in her apartment.

"You said come in, Katie, so here I am." He was drunk, she realized, and that meant dangerous. She glanced around for her phone and saw it sitting in the charger on the bedroom bureau, across the space. There was nothing in the bathroom within reach she could use as a weapon.

"You've been warned not to come back on lodge property. What do you want?"

Kay hoped if she sounded stern and scolding, she'd gain an advantage.

"I've been here all along, just nobody bothered to check I'd really gone. Lots of places on this land for a guy to hang and not be seen."

"So why come out now?"

"Oh please, after your little scene in the barn with Stuart the night of the storm, I just couldn't wait any longer. Watching you suck and fuck, hearing you yell and plead for him to fuck your ass, baby, I came in my jeans from two stalls away." He gave her a self-satisfied look, one that was meant to be demeaning.

Kay realized he was there for his turn, and her stomach soured. She tried to evaluate her options and didn't see many. He already knew she wouldn't shy away from physically protecting herself, so he'd be prepared if she lunged at him. In the back of her mind she wondered if Travis or Stuart would come look for her if she didn't show up. Maybe, she decided, but not for a while. In the meantime she had to outsmart this creep. She heard Stuart's dog at her door, giving her his occasional yip to be let in.

"Shut up your lousy dog," Jimmy hollered, and she hoped someone else in the complex would hear. When the dog barked, he took a small wooden box she kept earrings in on the top of her bureau and threw it at the door. "Go away," he screamed.

"I'll get him," she said in a low tone. "If I don't pet him, he won't go away." Drawing a breath, she slithered past him and headed to the door. He grabbed her upper arm, holding her in place.

"Where do you think you're going? You're mine tonight."

"I know that, Jimmy, but if I don't get rid of the dog, someone else might hear." She hoped she sounded somewhat interested in his attentions and smiled at him. "Relax, have a drink. There's a bottle of vodka in the mini-fridge in the corner."

"Don't try anything stupid, Kay. I know this land like the back of my hand. You have no place to hide."

"I understand," she mumbled and pointed him toward the small fridge. Kay opened the door and bent down to pet the dog. As she did, she grabbed several of her earrings that had landed in the doorway and wrapped them around his collar. As if she were ruffling the dog's ears, she took a few more and wrapped them around the leash clasp.

"That's enough. You should be hugging me."

Kay slowly stood and looked at the dog. "Go to Stuart, go on, leave me alone." It took all her strength not to vault after the animal and run for her life, but she knew Jimmy was within reach of grabbing her. If she pissed him off, it would be worse. "See, all he wanted was a quick pet and he's gone. Now, did you pour us a drink?"

She tried for casual and froze when he used his arm to wipe off all the items she kept on her bureau. Jumping when the clattering noise hit, she hoped someone downstairs heard and would come looking for her. In the meantime, she had to stay calm and outwit this lunatic.

"Where were you staying, Jim? You mentioned you stayed on the land and nobody knew you were here." She took a step inside but left the door cracked. "Aren't you going to get us a drink?"

Timms turned, and she saw her break. Kay didn't think or breathe—she yanked on the door handle and pulled it inward, making her getaway. She prayed he'd not catch her, but he was right behind her, grabbing at her hair as she hit the top of the outer staircase. She screamed involuntarily, and he twisted harder, dragging her back up the steps toward her apartment. He was screaming, his words not understandable, only that she'd pissed him off. In a fleeting glance, she saw Martha push the kitchen curtain aside. Kay yelled for help, with her full voice. She remembered tumbling down the staircase and landing in a heap at the bottom, but everything went black after that.

Kay woke cradled against Stuart's chest, his arm protectively around her, his hand pushing the hair from her face.

"Timms," she managed, and he pulled her tighter.

"Don't worry, he's gone. Just relax. Are you hurt?"

"I don't know," she said with a nervous laugh, noticing the rest of the employees standing around them. Martha knelt down and pressed a cold cloth to her forehead. "I think I'm okay," she added, suddenly embarrassed by all the staff watching her. In the distance she could hear a siren getting closer, and she relaxed back against Stuart.

"Do you want me to call the emergency for you?" The look on his face showed true angst. She realized in that instant he truly did care.

"No, I don't think so. Let's see if I can stand first." There were several suggestions from the staff about letting her get up or not, but she slowly maneuvered her body one limb at a time until she first sat forward. Her head spun a bit, but she held the cloth to her forehead.

With Stuart's help, she stood and got her footing. "I think I'm okay, I'm just pissed."

"I know, Kay, we'll talk about Timms later. For now, are you all right?"

"I think so. I'd like a drink, but this time I do want to press charges against Timms." She stretched her neck and straightened her clothing. "I think I'm all put together." Turning to Martha, she smiled. "Thanks for the cold cloth. I don't feel like it needs stitches. I think it's just a bump."

"A bump that blacked you out for minutes, Kay, long minutes."

"I'll be okay, better when I get Timms in a cell. Where is he?"

"Hoyt and Travis have him tied up in the bunkhouse kitchen. Sheriff is on his way."

"Good, I want to talk to the sheriff. Stuart, did you know all this time he's been living on the lodge land?" He looked appalled at the concept. "I think he's been staying in the storage sheds. He claims…" Kay glanced around and looked to Martha. "I know it's an imposition, but would you mind making a pot of coffee?"

"Of course, it's already brewing. You could use a couple of aspirin too. Come inside, into the living room." Kay let Martha begin to lead her inside, rolling her eyes at Stuart, hoping he'd get the message that she wanted to talk to him privately.

"All right, everyone inside, I'm sure the police will want to take statements. Let's all just settle down." Martha's directions were followed without question. "Come on all of you, give them a minute."

Kay watched as the staff wandered into the house and sighed in relief when they were finally gone.

"We'll be there in just a minute, Martha. Please get Kay some aspirin and make sure Hoyt and Travis have Timms securely tied."

Martha turned to enter the main bunkhouse and gave him a wave of her hand. "He's secure, but I'll get the aspirin. I'm sure Kay could use a hug and without an audience."

There were several groans and comments, but Martha reminded

the staff of the poker game they were playing when they heard the ruckus. That seemed to take the onus off Kay.

"Stuart, he was in the barn the night of the storm. He watched us…fuck. Started relating the details to me, telling me he wanted to reenact them."

"It's okay, we'll deal with him. Are you sure you want to go in there with him? I could carry you upstairs to rest."

"Oh no, I want to be in there when the sheriff comes to arrest him."

"Kay, this is all my fault in too many ways. I'm sorry he hurt you."

"Technically, I think I hurt myself more when I fell on the steps."

"Martha said he was dragging you by your hair and you were struggling to get free."

"Yes, I was trying to get away. The idea he thought he could touch me the way you did was revolting. I knew from the look on his face he'd hurt me, Stuart, in more ways than I care to think about." She hesitated. "I should have pressed charges the last time and none of this would have happened. He's crazy, Stuart. He wanted to hurt me, and from his actions, he would have enjoyed it." An involuntary shudder ran through her. Stuart tightened his arm around her shoulder, and she leaned into his comfort.

"That won't happen now, I promise you. He's done enough to put him away without bail for a while. We'll make sure he's not let out for a long time."

"I'd appreciate that. I don't want to keep looking over my shoulder wondering if he's there, waiting to pounce."

"Don't even contemplate it. I promise that won't happen." The siren noise got closer, and Martha appeared in the doorway. "Martha has your aspirin. Give Timms a wide berth for now. Go inside, Kay, I want to talk to the sheriff."

"But…"

"Please, Kay, just this one time, do as I ask."

"I do want the aspirin," she said, leaving him alone outside as the police pulled into the lodge compound.

Kay took the aspirin with the offered glass of water and leaned on the kitchen counter, watching Timms from across the room. His hands were tied behind his back and his chest anchored with bungee cords to the wooden chair. Even his legs were tied together. He glared at her, and she refused to flinch. Instead, she stared directly at him and wondered who had given him the black eye and swollen lip.

"Thanks, guys," she said to all the men in the kitchen, not singling any one out. Hoyt stood beside him with his rifle in hand. Travis stood on the other side, his knuckles wrapped in a kitchen towel. She'd bet there were ice chips in it but didn't ask.

"You bitch," Timms slurred, and Kay caught him wink at her with a cynical smile.

"You weren't that drunk when you tried to rape me, Timms. Don't assume the sheriff will assume you were inebriated. I'll have him give you a breathalyzer for the record just to prove you were in your right mind."

"I should have just taken what I wanted. That damn dog."

"Precious dog," Kay answered, turning to see Stuart and the sheriff enter.

"Well now, what do we have here?" The sheriff's tone was all business. "Mr. Timms, to start with, you're trespassing among other things." He turned to Kay and gave her a once-over. "You okay, miss?"

"By the grace of God and the dog," she told him. "I'm okay but pissed. He's been on lodge land all this time, skulking around and watching me, spying on all of us."

"Sounds like stalking to me," he said and asked everyone to clear out of the kitchen. He sat at the table and invited Kay to sit. Martha made herself busy with coffee and cake while he took notes. She noted Stuart stood still in the doorway, crushing the band of his hat between his fingers when she relayed how she found Timms in her apartment and what he had in mind. Travis watched the whole scene through lidded eyes, and she understood he was the one who hit Timms. She'd have to thank him later.

"Well, Mr. Timms, it seems you have a lot on your plate right now." He glanced to Stuart. "Who does your background checks?" Stuart rattled off a security company name. "Well, I'd say it's time to get a new company. Seems Mr. Timms here has a lot more to his background than originally thought."

"What are you talking about?" Kay watched Stuart straighten and take the seat beside the sheriff.

"When the call came in about him tonight, I had the office run him for outstanding warrants. On deeper inspection, it seems Mr. Timms has several aliases and outstanding warrants in several states. He likes to use his fists to settle arguments. Your attempted rape, stalking, and trespassing are going to have to take a backseat to his manslaughter charges in New Mexico and the two armed robberies in Idaho. Seems he was convicted of the robberies and got away in transit to the state prison by assaulting an officer. That will be another charge added. The manslaughter charge came after the grand theft of a jewelry store in New Mexico went wrong."

Timms started struggling with his bonds when Travis moved behind him and wrapped his arm around the man's throat. "Try it, give me an excuse to snap your pathetic neck. Save a lot of states a lot of money prosecuting you and keeping your ass in jail for life." Kay saw him snug his arm up a bit tighter. "Sheriff, does New Mexico or Idaho have the death penalty, or will he rot in a cell for the rest of his life?" Kay noted the sheriff didn't answer, just nodded at Travis, who released his hold on Timms. He made a production of slumping back onto the chair.

"I think I have enough for now. Kay, Stuart, I'll need you both to come into the office tomorrow morning and make formal statements."

"No problem, we'll be there early. Any idea when his first court appearance might be?"

"We'll know that all tomorrow, after we're done processing him. He'll have a hearing here about these charges. In the meantime, I'll let the district attorney contact the other states and see what they want to do about extradition."

"Thank you, Sheriff. I appreciate your help. I'll sleep better knowing he's in a cell tonight." Kay stepped forward and shook his hand.

"You'll be safe tonight. He isn't going anywhere. Just for general principles, Ms. Farrell, let the deputy take a few photos of that knot on your head and the bruises on your arm."

"Of course," she said and understood the more evidence, the better the case against him. She felt humiliated sitting in the brightly lit kitchen and posing for the deputy to photograph the knot on her head and the bruises starting to show on her upper arm. Stuart and the sheriff had walked outside, Travis following as Timms was led out in handcuffs.

The next hour was a blur for a bit, everyone hovering and wanting to hear what they missed. Travis stepped back inside and sent everyone on to their evening activities. They were asked to be careful what they said to any media outlets that might ask for statements, reminding them their paychecks depended on the lodge maintaining its reputation in all directions.

Finally, with the crew dispersed, Travis took Kay by the hand and mentioned to Martha they were heading to the office. She nodded and went about cleaning up her kitchen. Kay was thankful she'd slipped away to freshen up and change her clothes while the sheriff was downstairs. It was silly, but she felt safer jumping in the shower while he was in residence. It was a quick transformation, but at least she felt almost human again. Her head throbbed slightly, and her whole body ached where she'd hit each wood riser as she tumbled down the steps. She stood and walked beside Travis, holding her head high, wanting to crumble in his arms as soon as they were out of sight.

They'd rounded the corner of the building, out of anyone's sight, when he pulled her against his chest. "Kay, I'm so sorry. If I never brought you here, this wouldn't have happened."

"This is not your fault—it's Timms's fault for being a scumbag and trying to hide here at the lodge. Besides, I'd not have missed this time working with you for anything."

She felt her cheeks heat and knew they were turning shades of red. "And the sex wasn't bad either."

She tried to laugh, but he pulled her tighter and whispered, "I love you, darling, you know that. Whatever Stuart decides he wants, I'm always here for you…in my own way."

She pulled back and smiled. "You mean for friendship and sex but not for a commitment that includes the word marriage."

"Some dogs you can't teach new tricks."

"I like your tricks as they are and accept you as you are."

"Kay, if anything had happened, I would have had to hurt him."

"I know, Travis, and I appreciate it. And I'd condone it." They paused for a few seconds before they both started to smirk then finally laughed in relief. "Come on, let's go hear what Stuart has to decree."

At his office, it was clear he was agitated. Even old Harley seemed on alert, sitting by the desk instead of sprawled on the old leather sofa.

"Kay, I'm so sorry this happened. Are you sure you're all right, that you don't need medical attention?"

"I'm okay. A fall down the stairs won't stop me. And now that I know for sure Timms is gone I feel much better."

"How about a drink?" Travis asked and got a stern look from Stuart.

"Tomorrow, we'll all go to the sheriff's office for statements. I want you both in top shape in case he gets a lawyer with thoughts of getting him bail."

"We'll be ready," Travis offered. "Ah, before this all happened you wanted to see me and Kay. Want to tell us what that was about?"

Stuart looked confused for a moment and shook it off. "That

doesn't matter right now. Best we take care of Timms first. Why not get some sleep, Kay. Tomorrow will be a long day, and you'll probably be sore from your fall." He was distracted, she noted, his fingers flexing and the vein in his temple throbbing prominently.

"Okay, you'll let us know what you wanted when things settle down."

"Do you want to stay in the main lodge tonight instead of going back to your apartment?"

"'No, I don't feel threatened anymore. I'll be fine. I guess I'll see you both in the morning." She paused and bent to hug the dog, staying to untangle her favorite silver chandelier earring from his collar.

"That was a good idea, Kay. We saw the jewelry on his collar just as Martha called to tell us there was a problem."

"Timms knocked the box to the floor. I was more surprised that Harley showed up when he did. It's like the dog had some kind of ESP."

"Whatever he has, I'm glad he's around." Travis's voice broke with emotion, and he left the office quickly.

"Well, emotion from Travis, you guys really are upset. I'm okay, really. He didn't hurt me."

"We all are upset, Kay. This could have ended much differently."

"I know, Stuart. Trust me, I know. When I found him in my apartment, I got sick. When he started telling me how he watched us fuck and would do the same, I knew I couldn't let him take me. I guess I'm just too stubborn."

"While I hate your stubborn streak in many ways, tonight it came in handy." He took a step toward her, his hand rising, but he stopped short of touching her. "Let's get this all settled. Call if you need anything tonight." He turned and left her alone in his office.

"Well, I guess I've been dismissed." She petted the dog a bit longer before heading back to her apartment.

Chapter Nineteen

Kay was exhausted when they finally returned to the lodge. She had been prepared for a long day, but not for the way Timms was represented at his hearing. To hear his lawyer's version, she was a slut who invited him to her bed. As for the charges in the other states, they claimed it was a case of mistaken identity. Thankfully, fingerprints and photographic proof were enough to have the local judge hold him without bail for two weeks until both sides had more time to flush out the truth. She didn't want to think about his being let out on bail. She'd have to leave the lodge and flee the state to get away from Timms.

The DA assured her he was in contact with the New Mexico authorities and would straighten it all out before the next hearing. He was determined to extradite Timms out of state to pay for previous crimes. She had his assurances she'd be kept apprised of the situation. Kay decided this was all out of her hands now, and worrying about it wouldn't help her. At least for two weeks she could relax. And she'd make damn sure she was in the courtroom for the next hearing.

She'd skipped supper and went directly to swim, hoping to lose the angst building inside her. It didn't matter how many laps she swam, only that she was beginning to feel human again, like her old self. The knot on her head had changed color but didn't ache unless she touched it. Her arm was bruised, but she'd survive. It had been a difficult day, but Stuart never left her side. Neither did Travis. She decided whatever happened between them, she valued each man for his attention to her. Even if they never had sex again, they both proved to be protective men.

She'd been lost in her thoughts and hadn't heard the men enter the pool enclosure. Travis's clearing his throat when she reached the far end of the concrete hole got her attention.

"Hi," she managed, and pushed off to swim toward them. "What are you two up to?" she asked, watching them from the water.

"You haven't eaten today; we decided it was time to feed you." Travis laughed and moved to the ladder with a toweling robe in his hand, reaching it toward her. She took it and wrapped herself in it, using a second towel to blot her hair.

"I am getting hungry," she admitted. "Do I have time to wash the chlorine off?" Not waiting for an answer, she headed to the far end of the enclosure and turned on the fresh water shower. She hung the robe on the hook and stepped under the spray, letting it wash down over her hair and body. She had no second thoughts about tugging off her wet bathing suit before leaving the warm water and tying the robe around her a second time. "Am I cooking?" she asked, watching both men for some sign of what they had in mind.

"Let's meet in my office," Stuart said, not bothering to hide his outright appraisal of her. "We never did get to have our conversation last night." He strode from the area without looking back.

"Come on, I'll wait with you while you change." Travis handed her a dry towel.

"Any idea what this is all about?" They headed toward the apartments, both speculating about Stuart's need to talk.

"No idea. He had one of the staff make some sandwiches. Other than that, I'm as clueless as you are."

"Well, better to find out than wonder."

Travis waited in her apartment while she changed into dry clothes. She ran a comb through her wet hair but didn't bother to dry it, opting to let it air dry on the walk over.

"Want a drink before we go?" she asked, but Travis shook his head no.

"Best just to get this all out in the open. I can usually figure out what's on his mind, but this time I'm clueless."

When they entered the office, she saw Stuart had his back to the door, looking out the window. Travis nodded to a rolling cart with several platters of food waiting for them. He spoke without turning.

"Help yourselves," Stuart told them but didn't budge.

"Later. I'd rather have a drink." Travis moved to the bar and picked up the vodka carafe. Kay nodded her acceptance, and he assumed for Stuart. After pouring three glasses, he wandered back and handed one to Kay and the other to Stuart, rousing him from his thoughts. Kay glanced to Travis when Stuart emptied his in one long pull and walked back to the bar, refilling his glass. He started back toward them and hesitated, taking the container with him.

Kay sat on the leather sofa, Harley stretched out beside her, accepting his ear rub. Travis was propped on the arm of the sofa. Stuart sat on the low coffee table before them and put the vodka down within reach.

"You wanted to see us last night," Travis started but stopped short when Stuart put his hand up to ward off his question.

"All right. I can't keep going on like this. I'm truly sorry about Timms hurting you, Kay, in many ways. Beyond it happening on my land, twice, I should have known better."

"How could you? You did a background check on him. What else were you supposed to do?"

"Make sure he was off my land."

"Well, that's done now, and from the sounds of it today, he'll be out of our state soon." Travis reached down and clasped Stuart's shoulder. "What did you want last night?"

"It seems I've been very closed-minded. I've realized of late that I don't want Kay to go to Seattle when her contract is up."

Travis turned to Kay. "Are you going to leave?"

"I figured it would be best for all of us. I was going to talk to you about it after my vacation. I wanted to scope things out first, but yes, I decided to move on. I don't want to be the cause of tension between you two."

"Honey, you cause tension when you walk in a room," he teased. "I was hoping you'd extend your contract. I just got things running well. The rest of the staff like you, and more important, they respect you. Hell, I wanted to make you second on a permanent basis."

"I'd like that too, Travis, but it's not fair to Stuart to be on edge on his land and in his business."

"Well, that's the point. I have been on edge. You are one tough woman, Kay, in too many ways to recount. You drive me crazy at every turn, but the idea of not seeing you every day is worse. I've decided if you'll stay, I'll go along with your point of contention."

"What?" Kay finished her drink but held the glass between her hands. "I thought you weren't into me or my lifestyle."

"I wasn't. But I've come to realize it was because it was your idea and not mine that bothered me more. Hell, Travis and I have shared women in the past. I just didn't want to share you with anyone. But, if it means keeping you here at the lodge on a permanent basis, I have a counteroffer."

"I'm listening," she managed, not prepared for this. In the back of her mind she was ready for him to ask her to leave.

"You and Travis can work out your business end of the kitchen. Whatever works for both of you. I've even thought about taking a small storefront in town for you to open your bakery." He paused and sipped his drink. "And if it takes bringing Travis into our sex life to keep you here, I'd rather share you with him than any other man. At least with Travis, we understand each other."

Kay deliberately put her glass on the table beside him before she dropped it. She glanced to Travis, who seemed stunned, then back to Stuart. Several things ran through her mind, and she wasn't sure what to focus on, which left her staring at Stuart, dumbstruck.

"What, no witty comeback?"

"You have to admit it came from left field. I'm gearing up to move on, and now you tell me you've decided you'll let me have my way? What changed, what was the catalyst?"

"You knew when you told me you were ready to move on because I was a tight ass, I'd have to make a choice. I've decided to accept your contention. Quite frankly, after our night in the barn, you've got me wondering if I could satisfy you on my own." He gave a half laugh, but it fell flat.

"Why would you think you wouldn't be enough? From that performance I was impressed. And just to be clear, I wanted to be honest with you about Travis. I enjoy him and occasionally still want to fuck him. But I figured it would be better to do it with you than behind your back."

"Anyone want my opinion?" Travis interceded.

He got a stern no from Kay and at the same time, Stuart shot him a dirty look.

"Travis, are you interested in joining Stuart and me in bed occasionally? Will it bother you if I start a relationship with Stuart? I know our situation will never go anywhere beyond just friendship and sex, so why shouldn't I have the freedom to enjoy you both?"

"I think we're overthinking this way too much. I think," he walked toward the office door and flipped the lock, "we should just go with the mood and forget about tomorrow for now." On his way back, he paused to pull the heavy drapes closed over the windows. One last detour to the desk, and he took the receiver from the desk phone. He pulled his cell from his pocket and made a production of turning it off. Stuart watched his moves and reached into his shirt pocket, tossing his phone to him. When it was turned off and placed on the desk, Travis walked toward them and took several condoms from his wallet, tossing them on the desk. Then he sat beside Stuart on the coffee table. "Well, what would you like?"

"Maybe we called her bluff," Stuart added, his tone shaky.

"Not my bluff," she told him and gave both men a complete look-over. "Stand and drop the pants, boys, I want to suck your cocks." She made a show of tugging the hem of her shirt up and over her breasts, tossing it aside. Next came her bra, which she threw aside. Kay raised her hands to her breasts and massaged them. "God, that feels so much better—metal and skin shouldn't mix."

Tweaking her own nipples, she watched as the men toed off their shoes. Travis was naked movements later, his hand stroking his erection. Stuart took a bit longer, his mood seemingly confused. Licking her lips, she reached to Travis and moved him by his hips to stand before her. Kay took his cock between her lips and savored his bulk. Remembered his taste and scent and sighed. She reached for Stuart, who stood rooted to the spot, and pulled him beside Travis by his cock. He jerked forward and came to stand shoulder to shoulder with the other man. With a hand on each cock, she stroked both men, taking turns to suck their cock heads or nip their bases. She'd take one long pass of Travis' cock, swallowing it down her throat, and repeat the same on Stuart.

Kay didn't know how long they stayed there and didn't care. What mattered were these two amazing men letting her love them without guilt. Stuart laced his fingers in her almost dry hair when she took his cock between her lips.

"That's it, Kadence, suck me down your throat."

"Let's move to the desk," Travis suggested. He left Kay with Stuart's cock to suck while he cleared off the desktop. When it was empty he walked to Kay and reached for her hand. As she stood, he dropped his head and captured one of her nipples between his teeth. Stuart followed suit and started sucking and massaging her other. She heard her own groan of approval and wrapped a hand behind each man's neck, holding them tight to her.

"That's amazing," she told them and continued to hold them to her breasts. Travis reached to pinch her buttocks while Stuart used both his hands to pump her tit. Her nipples were hard and puckered, her breasts heavy with need. Kay knew her pussy was wet, would be hot to the men's touch. That spurred her to move their positions.

She reluctantly dropped her hands and led them behind the desk.

She sat in the desk chair and prompted them to lean side by side on the desktop. The position left her at the perfect height to suck them.

When it was her idea, she loved to suck a man's cock. When it was expected, the act annoyed her. Tonight she was in heaven, swapping back and forth between their stiff dicks. She tasted their first drops of pre-cum, noting how they tasted different. "Travis, you taste spicy, like thyme and sage." She paused to lick Stuart's. "You taste like whiskey. All very interesting."

"What does your pussy taste like, Kay?" Travis asked.

"I guess you'll have to decide for yourself, later, after I make you come on my tits and you lick it off. Then you can do anything you want to me." She dropped to her knees from the chair and started sucking both men in earnest, milking their cocks down her throat and stroking them with a hit of her fingernails to their skin.

"I'm going to come, Kay," Travis told her, and she focused on him, handling Stuart while she nipped at Travis's cock base, biting lightly. When his cock surged, she pulled away and directed his cum toward her tits. Her hand continued to pump him dry as she went back to Stuart's and repeated the process. He too came on her tits.

After licking them both clean, she sat back on her heels and rubbed their cum into her skin. Travis reached down and lifted her to rest on the desk. Stuart was at her breast in an instant, licking her clean. Travis winked at her just before his head descended to her other nipple.

"Rub your pussy, Kay." Stuart's request was muffled as he didn't let go of her nipple.

She let her hand drop to her crotch and began rubbing the heel of her hand against herself.

"That's not right, you should be naked so you can finger fuck yourself."

"I would be, but I don't want either of you to stop sucking my tits."

"We'll get back there," Travis said, reaching down to undo her jeans. Stuart let go of his hold and she sighed in disappointment until he lifted her by the waist. Travis tossed her clogs to the side and pulled her jeans and panties down her legs and off. He left her standing before them, her hands keeping her balance on their shoulders while they went back to her breasts. They each used their hands to roam her body. Stuart dropped his to her crotch and ran his fingers along her pussy lips. Travis's large hand was pumping her ass cheek.

"Damn, you are hot to my touch, girl," Stuart told her. He watched her face as he slid one finger between her pussy lips. She arched her back in acceptance.

"Another one, please." He smiled and slid a second finger in her pussy. "That's better, as a start."

"How about this?" Stuart asked as he dropped before her and began to lick her pussy.

"That's much better," she managed, her hand capturing her lonely breast and tugging on her nipple. Travis took her other hand in his and moved it to her other breast.

"Play here," he told her and dropped behind her. Kay let him move her slightly until her weight was settled a shoulder width apart. She finally found her version of heaven. Stuart sucked and fingered her pussy while Travis licked her anus and began to penetrate it with his finger. Kay pinched her tits hard and came around their fingers, her shudder unmistakable.

"That was amazing. Now who's going to fuck me and where?" She held back a smile as the two men pulled from her body.

"On your back, over the desk," Stuart said and left her pussy. He grasped her by the waist and hefted her up on his shoulder in a fireman carry until he reached his desk, gently lowering her. "Suck on Travis while I finger you a bit more."

She crooked her finger at Travis, who was already on his way to meet her lips. Kay loved the idea of having two men fill her. Travis was hard again and starting to release droplets of pre-cum. She knew she'd have to change the dynamics or he'd come before fucking her.

"Travis, switch places with Stuart. It's been ages since you licked me."

"Your wish," he teased, taking Stuart's place while he moved toward her mouth. Kay loved the way Travis licked her, fast and slow, sucking her clit and fingering her until she came. "I've got to fuck you, Kay, or I'll lose my load." He left her to suck Stuart and grabbed the condoms. She reached to help him with it, but he shook his head. "I'm too close," Travis told her, pushing in her pussy in one smooth stroke. She began to suck Stuart in the same rhythm Travis fucked her. Soon she felt her orgasm building inside her, but she wanted more.

Kay let go of Stuart's cock and ruffled Travis' hair. "I want to change positions." Both men seemed to understand and took a step back. She grabbed Stuart's hand and dragged him toward the coffee table, pausing only long enough to cover his cock with a condom. "Lie down, Stuart, let me straddle you." Kay decided he was still a bit in shock, quiet with his eyes wide, taking her instructions without comment. When she was settled with his cock buried in her pussy, she motioned to Travis, who had been standing to the side, fisting his erection. "You, in my ass, please."

"Whatever the lady wishes." He laughed as he snugged up behind her, taking long licks against her anus before edging his cock in her. "Damn, you'd be tight without his cock in your pussy. Now you're just…"

"Horny and in need. Don't be gentle, Travis, just stuff your cock in my ass and fuck me while Stuart is in my pussy. That's what I want, to feel both of you inside me at the same time."

Stuart held her tight at the waist while she leaned over his chest, sliding his hands higher to fondle her tits. "Christ, Kay, are you sure?" Stuart asked, nuzzling her breasts when she rose forward to give Travis better access to her ass.

"Definitely. I've wanted both of you to fuck me this way since the day I saw your photo under the lodge sign."

"Like this?" Travis asked as he fitted his cock fully inside her. "Is this what you've been fantasizing about all this time?"

"Yes, God help me, yes. I've wanted you both at the same time. I want you to do anything and everything we can together, every way we can."

"You were tight before, but with both our cocks in you I don't know how long I'll last."

Stuart seemed concerned, and she leaned down. "Pinch my nipples, bite them, Stuart, that will make me come. Then I'll let you guys come."

As they followed her directions, she felt her body react, knew she was sucking their cocks deeper inside her. Stuart came first, surging in her pussy, making her feel even fuller. That sent Travis over the edge. For a few blinding seconds, both men were coming inside her. Kay had never felt so full, even with toys. Live men were much better to play with, and her body quaked with her own orgasm.

They were all quiet for a few minutes, garnering their breath. Finally she felt Travis's thighs start to tremble, and he pulled from her anus. With his hands around her waist, he helped her to stand over Stuart and lifted her from his cock. He took a few steps back and rested both their weight on the desk.

"That was amazing," she told them.

Stuart lifted his head only a few inches before dropping it back to the table. Travis held her tighter and laughed.

"So that's what it takes to satisfy you now?" He squeezed her breast, and she sighed.

"Go figure, who'd have known I needed two hard cocks to make me come?"

"Stuart, I think you were right. The only way we'll survive her is if we do it together."

"Truer words, my friend. I admit I need help with her."

"You poor guys, having to put so much effort into fucking me."

"A cross I'll learn to bear," Stuart admitted. He finally stretched and stood. She watched as he tossed his used condom in the wastebasket and smiled when he moved before her and wrapped his fingers around her tit. "Travis, what do you think? Can the two of us keep her satisfied?" He leaned down and licked her nipple. "Maybe she needs to be spanked?" His cock stirred, and Kay laughed aloud.

"Just remember, what's good for one is good for all of us."

"I'm not sure I like the glint in her eyes just now." Stuart looked to Travis. "I think I might have opened a doorway."

Kay reached down and stroked his stirring cock. "Just one door. I've got a lot more ideas to experiment with."

"Death by sex," Stuart mused, glancing to Travis.

"I'll die trying to satisfy her," Travis told him, finally releasing his hold on her.

She dropped her hands and took a step back, standing tall and leaning into a stretch of her full naked body. "I'll die if I don't get something to eat soon. Food first, then round two, boys."

Leaving left the warmth of their arms, Kay reached down to grab Stuart's button-down shirt. She made sure to have her back to them when she did and got the anticipated groan from her men. "Later, guys. Feed me, then we'll switch places. Travis, I want to suck you while Stuart fucks my ass."

Kay heard her words, knew they sounded so matter-of-fact, and realized she'd finally found what she'd been searching for. Two amazing men who would fuck her until she couldn't come anymore.

Epilogue

Kay lay exhausted over Travis's chest while Stuart thrust a few last times before pulling from her anus and dropping to their side. They lay quiet for a few moments until she finally found enough energy to lift her weight from Travis and let his deflating cock slide from her pussy. She tucked herself between the two men and reached a hand to each of their bellies.

"Thank you," she said, while stretching her whole body.

"You're welcome," Stuart offered and rolled onto his side, his fingers trailing over her breast, prompting her nipple to bud.

"Next time," Travis broke in, finally sitting forward and rolling his head on his neck to stretch out the kinks, "could we at least wait until the windows are installed?" He waited a few seconds before he started to laugh. "At least could we bring a blanket or two to lie on?"

"Hey, I told Kay it would be cold and hard and she said she'd warm us both up."

"Well she did manage to do that," Travis conceded.

"And neither of you complained at the time." She stood and started to wander around the empty room. "Who knew you'd want the comfort of heat and beds. I said I wanted to come and christen the new house."

"Yes, you did." Stuart laughed. "But let's wait until the house is dried in before we do this again.

"And the counters are in, then you can bend me over them and fuck me from behind."

"That sounds like a plan," Stuart said, finally rising and going to the pile of their clothing. He grabbed his flannel shirt and dropped it over her shoulders.

"Where am I in this scenario?" Travis asked.

"How about sitting on the counter so I can suck you while Stuart fucks me?"

"That will work, or some version of it."

Kay leaned down and reached for his hand, helping him to stand. When the three of them were standing before the opening where the picture window over the kitchen sink would soon sit, she grasped each man's cock and started to stroke them. "Are you sure it's too cold here?"

Kay watched her men glance to one another and smile. "What the hell, we'll make our own warmth." Stuart grabbed her around the waist and hoisted her up on his shoulder. "Come on, the bedroom windows are in, it will be warmer in there."

"Now he tells us there's a room with windows!" Travis followed after pausing to retrieve the wine they had been sharing to christen Stuart's new home.

"This is very different from the original plans you showed me." Kay looked around the empty master bedroom space as Stuart gently set her to stand.

"Yeah, well Travis and I had a few thoughts on that. We've decided it will take both of us to satisfy you completely full time. So, with a few changes in here, the master bedroom now has room for all three of us to live here comfortably."

She glanced from Stuart to Travis. "Are you both sure?"

"I am," Travis said. For the first time since she'd known him, he actually blushed, his neck and cheeks turning pink. "Look, I've always said I'm not a man of commitment, but this just feels right."

"Stuart?"

"Hell, I was never an ordinary kind of guy. The three of us together works. Why change it? Besides, with all the crazy hours we work, this just made sense. At least at night, when we can all finally relax, we'll be together."

"That's what you two decided?" She again searched their faces and noted they were both holding back smiles. "I think I'm very lucky to have two men who understand me so completely." She stretched to her full height and let Stuart's flannel shirt drop from her body. "Can you tell what I'm thinking now?" Kay used her hands to grasp her breasts, pinching her nipples until they were hard and puckered, noting both men's cocks were stirring back to life.

THE END

WWW.LOUISANEIL.COM
LOUISANEIL@ YAHOO.COM

ABOUT THE AUTHOR

Louisa became hooked on paperback romance novels as a teen. Before cable TV arrived, babysitting after school was boring. She chose a Harlequin novel and never looked back.

As an adult, she took writing seminars and classes to craft her own skills. She kept journals and notebooks filled with story ideas and bits of dialogue, along with settings and observations.

Finally retired from her full time job, she ventured to put her notes in order. The end result was *Claudia's Men*, her first romance novel with a twist.

She realized her writing stepped beyond normal boundaries and became erotica. Exploring these new directions has been enlightening in many ways. The author looks forward to researching her next ménage novel.

Also by Louisa Neil

Ménage and More: *Claudia's Men*
Ménage Amour: *The Stagers*
Ménage Amour: *Is Three A Crowd?*

Siren Publishing, Inc.
www.SirenPublishing.com